The Moment It All Changed

Short Stories of Adventure, Inspiration, Epiphany, Humor, and Surprise

Steven R. Roberts

iUniverse, Inc.
New York Bloomington

The Moment It All Changed
Short Stories of Adventure, Inspiration, Epiphany, Humor, and Surprise

iUniverse books may be ordered through booksellers or by contacting:

iUniverse
1663 Liberty Drive
Bloomington, IN 47403
www.iuniverse.com
1-800-Authors (1-800-288-4677)

ISBN: 978-1-4502-6487-7 (sc)
ISBN: 978-1-4502-6490-7 (dj)
ISBN: 978-1-4502-6489-1 (ebk)

Printed in the United States of America

iUniverse rev. date: 10/19/2010

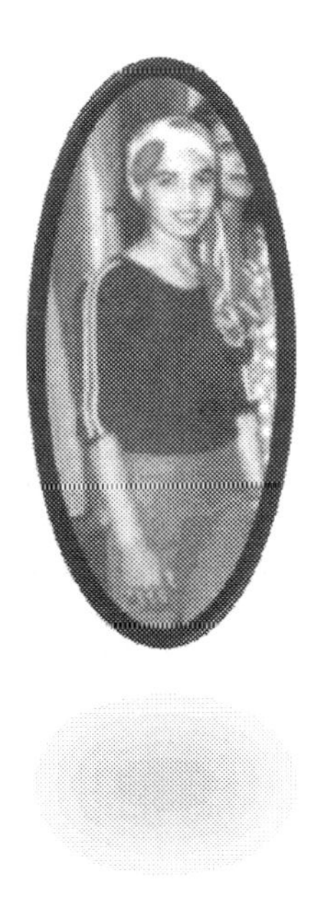

Miriam the night before the trip.

"Muchachos, me voy para El Yuma."

("Boys, I'm going to America")

Miriam Serrano

This anthology of short stories is dedicated to my mother,
Marguerite Roberts, who left us in May, 2009.
Mom was a great story teller.

Acknowledgements

Thanks to the many individuals who provided the inspiration for, and in some cases, the writing of, these short stories. Thanks go out to Miriam Serrano for our luncheon meetings where she described her life leading up to the miracle voyage captured in *Miriam's Miracle*; to Rollin Kerzee for our times together discussing the events that led to the true story of the *Family Fire;* to Tom Gerbec for the inspirational story about his "Gramps", *The Carpathian Cook;* and to Bob Blackman for accompanying me to Scotland and the dream included in *A Hacker Plays The Big Ones.*

A special thanks goes to the late David Wood who, during his 92nd year on this earth, made me feel I'd known him his whole life. Before he left us in January, 2009, our discussions had formed the basis for the true story, *Cold Hayride,* included in this book as well as the novel, *A Freak's Journey,* released in February, 2010.

Thanks also to the guest storytellers, Chrissie Bowman, Pierette Simpson, Shirley Cheng, and Carl Steinhouse. Brief bios for these guest authors are included at the end of their contributions.

A special thanks goes to my wife, Jane, for reading and editing many drafts of the book as well as adding substance to the stories. To Joan Saynor, Dixie Cotner and Peggy Tucker go my thanks for reading the manuscript and correcting my sometimes sideways spelling, grammar and punctuation. And thanks to Sandra Richardson for sprinkling punctuation and grammar all over the manuscript and otherwise professionally editing the draft. Thanks also to iUniverse for their helpful Editorial Evaluation. In the end, however, any misguided commas, letters or words that made it into print are my responsibility.

Foreword

This collection of short stories about events that changed people's lives is dedicated to those who not only survived but thrived in reacting to such moments. These events may well happen every day someplace in the world but in these cases they happened to someone you will soon know. The idea is to provide the entertainment of a short story well told, introduce the reader to some colorful characters and vivid places and, in some instances, give a glimpse of a point of view or experience that may be off the normal radar screen.

"Thrashing, under the water and nearly naked, I banged my head on one of the wheels. Trying desperately to find a pocket of air under the ice, I headed toward the front of the wagon instead of toward the hole."

David Wood
From *Cold Hayride*

Contents

A Short Word About Short Stories

Every day is a surprise. In the total scheme of our lives, however, the moments are mostly minor personal tragedies and adventures so we just keep on keepin' on. The boss assigns a new pile of work. Your wife adjusts your priority list for the weekend. You win the football pool at work. Your teenaged son gets arrested for something stupid. Those to-die-for red shoes finally go on sale at Macy's. Your car disappears, never to be seen again in one piece. Your identity is stolen. Your best friend announces he is getting a divorce.

We tend to become numb to these daily happenings. Waking up in the morning, these events are not thought to be a part of the coming day. But when they are, we adjust our path to keep from getting too frustrated, excited or depressed, or just to avoid stepping knee deep in the doggy-doo that results. After all, we've got a life to live and we need to survive the day to live it.

Then there are the rare moments when an unexpected event happens and our lives are changed forever. Whether we realize it or not at first we are different from that moment forward and our attitude changes about an important concept, relationship or goal. The direction of our lives takes a turn sometimes for the better, sometimes for the worse.

The short story form used in this book, first given prominence in the mid 1800's, has many advantages in literature, particularly in today's busy world. The short story was first described and given life by Edgar Allan Poe in his 1842 critical review of Nathaniel Hawthorne's collection, *Twice Told Tales*. Poe was impressed with the power of unity and length of the short story form. In the review he said:

> "In almost all classes of composition, the unity of effect or impression is a point of greatest importance. It is clear, moreover that this unity cannot be thoroughly preserved in productions whose perusal cannot be completed at one sitting."

Poe also included in the critique:

> "The ordinary novel is objectionable, from its length.... As it cannot be read at one sitting, it deprives itself, of course, of the immense force derivable from totality."

The Moment It All Changed is an anthology of short stories about people standing, accidently or on purpose, in the path of a speeding train of circumstances and how they face the moment. Most of the tales are based on actual events but a few are not. I'm confident the difference will be clear.

In addition to those I've written, four stories by talented guest storytellers have been included. Their work adds an interesting variety of style and perspective.

Okay, here we go. Let's take off for some new places and meet some new people.

Miriam's Miracle

By Steven R. Roberts

The sea was quiet and the water was as black as the horizon and surely as black as the sky. What made me think I could do this, I wondered? Twenty men and I had been at sea for what seemed like four or five hours. Actually, no one had a watch so we really didn't know how long we'd been rowing that night. Each of us had left everything and everyone behind. Our fragile dreams for a better life this night were floating in a 20-foot, tar-covered row boat miles from the nearest shore.

It was an easy date to remember, 01-19-1991, my lucky number but I must admit I didn't plan it that way. It just happened. The boat was home-constructed by my college classmates; none of them had ever been to sea let alone known anything about boat design and construction. We were on our way north out of east Havana from the Cuban paradise we loved, a paradise where secrecy and show had been the foundation of Castro's communist government for 32 years. He'd been in control longer than any of us had been alive.

"Left," I shouted into the thick night air. I held the compass tightly and faced backwards from the bow as a gentle breeze picked up from our left. The little round dial I held with both hands was the only thing keeping us from circling around until we went down at sea or all succumbed to exposure and died in the boat. Most had at least one bottle of water but only a few had food, thinking the trip was an overnight journey despite our primitive form of transportation.

Looking back at the small boat load of Cubans trying to find a better place I wondered what America would think of us. Most of us had college degrees, over half had Masters, but we were a rag tag looking group for sure. I was wearing faded denim shorts torn a little at one pocket, a blue top with white stripes down the sleeve. I had worn my favorite orange and white bandana to keep my hair out of my eyes during the trip. We all wore our old clothes, leaving our better things behind for our families. Most of us were barefooted.

"Jorge, you are always too slow. Either row faster or let one of the others take your spot," I said. Jorge was the shortest but the most committed to the trip. He had been anxious to get out of Cuban's autocratic life and the first to volunteer for the risky trip.

"Enrique, wake up and take Jorge's spot."

"I wasn't sleeping, Miriam," Enrique said. "I couldn't sleep when my mind is going so many miles an hour."

"What are you thinking so much about, Enrique?" I asked.

"I am going to go to a big American market store and buy anything I want," Enrique said, stepping over and around two sets of legs and feet to exchange places with Jorge. "I hear they have hundreds of things in those big American stores."

"You can buy anything you want only if you have money," Renee said, "and you have none. Enrique, I think you will get skinny in the land of the north."

"I'm thinking of going to one of those hair parlors I saw in an old magazine and getting my hair styled," I said, pulling off my bandana and letting my long black hair fall over my shoulders. I tilted my head like a magazine model. My dream was undoubtedly unique among those of us in the boat that night. We had fallen into pointless small talk to keep our minds off the danger and fatigue of rowing out in the middle of the sea with the darkness closing in on all sides.

"Quiet," I said. "Listen… Hear it?" The six boys working the oars stopped mid strokes and we drifted quietly on the mild, rolling sea. We could hear the distant rumble of a power boat getting louder. I closed my eyes and listened for the arrival of the devil boat. Had I bullied my friends into leaving it all for a life in Havana's stinking prisons?

We had all been born into the paradise of Cuba so we had never known anything other than complete governmental control over our lives. Like so many young people in Cuba, I had personally seen the effects of living the hopeless, dependant life. Educated and out of work for several years, my father left home when I was two months old. Mother left five years later, leaving me to be raised by my grandparents. Grandma Lu and Grandpa Pucho had 10 children of their own still living at home when my brother, Tony, sister Margarita, and I moved into their home in east Havana. Pucho, who I called Pa, worked as a security guard at a plastics factory and Lu kept the house and watched after the 13 kids ranging in age from 3 to 25. With my siblings and aunts and uncles to play with there were always games and sports and minor skirmishes going on from morning till night.

Castro's government controlled everything from education to food consumption. The government prescribed how much of each main type of food (beef, rice, pork, beans) a family could eat each week. We had a government-issued small ledger advising when we could go to the government-owned store and pick up each item. The food rations per family kept us thin but alive.

One day my grandmother sent me and my friend, Olga, to get our allotment of beef.

"Here's the coupon book. Make sure you don't lose it," Lu said.

Olga was anxious to go with me so she could see a cute boy working at one of the nearby shops.

I claimed the heavy package and the butcher marked the family's coupon book. We giggled in front of the boy at the next shop and on the way home Olga and I talked about boys and other things young girls talk about when no one is listening. The package was heavy and when I got home I sat down on my bed, which was just inside the back door. I must have accidently kicked the package under my bed as I collapsed into a nap.

The next day Lu was racing from room to room looking all over the house for a dead animal. She found it under my bed.

"You foolish child," Pucho said when he came home from work. "Now, 15 people will have no beef this week because of your absentmindedness and stupidity."

"I didn't mean to do it, Pa," I cried. "I was tired and I forgot to put it in the refrigerator."

"Turn around and I'll help you remember to think about what you are doing," Pucho said.

I spent a week confined to my room lying on my bed, face down.

Being raised in a house of 13 children, seven boys and six girls offered us the choice of learning how to fend for ourselves against aggressors, or withdrawing and just observing the chaos. I was a bit shy with my new surroundings when I first moved in with my grandparents but a competitive, some might say aggressive, personality evolved by the time I came to the end of my stay and moved off to college.

When I was 16, a hard lesson of youth was learned about trust and self reliance from an incident involving a camping trip I organized for my high school class. We took a bus up the mountain and camped for two nights along the Compo Florido River. Despite being accompanied by school chaperones, dancing, partying and drinking went on into the night. I had little experience with drinking and I got pretty well bombed on crème de menthe. It tasted so good but I felt so sick the next morning that I didn't want to talk to any of the others at the camp. Olga couldn't stop laughing. She told me I had been the life of the party and had acted like a fool.

I confessed to Olga that I didn't really know what had happened on the mountain and I really had no idea how I had managed to get back to our tent. Returning to the city, I was so troubled about my behavior that I needed to confide in someone in the family. Aunt Tata had always listened to my little tragedies and personal problems as I was growing from child to woman, so I told her what had happened. I had her swear to secrecy because I knew Pucho would kill me if he found out I got drunk and couldn't remember what I was doing. Olga had also told me something about a boy being involved but luckily I didn't mention this to my aunt.

Later that day Tata went straight to Pucho and told him everything. My grandfather was waiting for me on the front porch when I got home from school. He stood as I walked up to the house causing me to take refuge in a wicker chair at the opposite end of the porch. Pa was wearing his security pistol even though he wasn't due at work until midnight.

"Keep your shoes on, girl, and stand up," he said, without looking at me. "We're going to take a little trip."

Pucho walked me back to school and down the hall to the principal's office where he made me apologize to Miss Sanchez for drinking and getting drunk on the school outing. Miss Sanchez didn't say much. She just smiled, looked at me and shook Pucho's hand and then we left. It was the most embarrassing moment of my teenage years and I didn't touch a drink again for a couple of weeks. I've stayed away from crème de menthe ever since.

I made it through high school and graduated with a "B-minus" average that translated to a 7.7 overall grade rating on the Cuban educational scale. My counselor told me before graduation that my rating left me 1.1 grade points below the level required to study my chosen field of Topography in college. I chose Telecommunication Engineering instead and entered the University in Cujay across town in Havana the following fall.

At Cujay, students spent the week at the University and went home on the weekends. As with many college freshmen, the new social freedom was exciting and filled with temptations. The dorm lights were turned off at 11 pm every night so the students could get a good night's sleep. That didn't really happen but that's another story.

Wonder of wonders, four years later I graduated with about the same grade performance as in high school. To continue my government-paid education I signed up for a Master's Degree in Engineering. The program involved two years of career-related national service combined with study. I was sent, along with four other students, 400 miles south to a rural community in Oriente Provence. Three days a week I spent from 8 am to 2:30 pm accompanying a telecommunication journeyman, observing and working on an actual job site. This was followed each day by sessions from 3 pm to 8 pm studying my major subjects.

I worked in the field for a man named Pupi, a name that brought grins from the two students who spoke English. He was originally from Haiti and he was so black he looked purple in the sunlight. Pupi gave out assignments each morning to the interns. Looking back, the technology was somewhat out of date and I remember stringing phone wires and even acting as a telephone operator at a switchboard.

There were many lessons learned on the job. One day while working in the office I received a quick lesson in employee relations. That particular day the tall, buxom office clerk and Juanita a feisty little brunet, both working for Pupi, discovered that he was sleeping with both of them.

"What the hell are you doing with my man?" Wanda, the ponytailed blond asked Juanita.

"Your man? I don't see no diamond," Juanita said, bending over Wanda's desk, maximizing her cleavage. "Seems to me you'd have a ring to show how good a lay you are."

"Why would the bastard come to me if you were any good in the dark?" ponytail asked.

"What about that, Pupi?" Juanita said, looking in the door of the boss's office where the boss and I were having a brief meeting. Pupi didn't seem to want to clarify the situation or try to calm things down. He shrugged his shoulders and raised his arms to the ceiling.

"Let them fight and they'll settle things just fine," he said to me. "I just want them to tell me who wins."

"You are a whore trying to sleep your way to a big bedroom," Wanda said. "I have more right than you to the bastard."

"Maybe our three-year-old son and the child I'm carrying should give me first rights to Pupi, no?" Juanita said.

That is the last day I saw Juanita at work.

I heard later that she and Pupi got married. No one from the office was invited to the wedding and Wanda quit the following week. I felt sorry for the three of them.

After two years in the field, I came back to Havana for a graduation ceremony at Cujay and a celebration at Lu and Pucho's house. I had completed my education according to Castro's plan and I decided to take a month off to rest before finding a job.

On a bright and breezy day in July, five classmates and I filed into the personnel office of the country's telephone company. The Personnel Director called all six of us in together and asked us to sit down. Our scholastic records were in folders lined up in a row on the front edge of his desk. He reviewed our educational history in the government system from elementary school through to our Master's Degrees.

"Congratulations to you, Mr. Ramirez. Your scholastic record is among the best I've seen," the Personnel Director said, standing, leaning over his desk to shake hands. He sat back down and proceeded to review each of the other files, each time shaking hands with the applicant and looking the young graduate in the eye, giving the same remark. In all honesty, I must confess that he wasn't quite as generous with praise after reviewing my file.

Finally he stood and walked to the window and held his hands together behind his back gazing out the window. His office overlooked the factory shop floor.

"The workers you can see from this window have jobs for life," he said. "We would have to lay off these long-time, experienced workers if we were to provide positions for inexperienced applicants. So you see, I'm sorry to say there are no jobs for you at this time."

Having gone through the government-provided education system for 18 years to get Master's Degrees, we were caught off guard and started to question the man's position.

"There are no jobs? What are we to do if the government cannot provide a job for us?" I asked. "It is your job to make jobs."

"Well, you will have to find jobs away from your majors until jobs requiring your skills open up," the Personnel Director said.

"The government approved our schools and major subjects for study," Renee said. "Why would they approve a field of study with no jobs at the end of the trail? Was our education just for show?"

"No," the man said. "There will be jobs but it will take time. I suggest you try construction or working in the government factories or stores until openings occur in your field."

"Digging in the ground was not one of our subjects," Nelson said. "You have to do something about this." Nelson was standing and shouting at the man."

"We will keep your applications in our files and advise you when openings occur. I'm afraid that is all we are authorized to do," the Personnel Director said as he directed us toward the door.

My classmates and I could see further debate was useless. We walked to a café for a coffee and sat in quiet disappointment and anger. After we had absorbed the news, we discussed our options. In Havana there are many people with government-funded college degrees and no jobs. The government pays for our mandatory education so they can boast of a 100% literate population, but it ignores its responsibility for creating work for the country's graduates. From the café we could see many checkers games going on in the square across the street. An ongoing joke about checkers and jobs in Havana was, "It's your move, Doctor." Were we to start playing checkers in the park in our early twenties?

I went home and told Lu the story of the meeting at the phone company.

"Something will come along," she said, which was her patient nature developed through raising thirteen children.

I was depressed and spent my days in the room I shared with my sister. Then I progressed into anger and I finally decided not to continue as a victim of Castro's regime. I invited my classmates and a few other close friends to a party in my grandparent's backyard. They gathered among the flowering bushes and trees that cut off the yard from the neighbors' views.

Grandmother Lu fixed a large batch of yellow rice with pork, beans, and tostones (fried green plantains). We added fried chips and filled a wash tub with cold beer.

The partygoers filled their plates with food and grabbed a beer, dispersing around the yard in groups of three or four. After the meal was finished and the guys were getting a second beer, I walked up two steps to the back porch. I rubbed my hands together as I always did when I gave presentations in class. Then I cleared my throat and spoke the words I had rehearsed in my mind for weeks.

"Muchachos, me voy para el Yuma," ("Boys, I am going to the America") I said, looking out over my guests, some of them stopping with forks midway to their mouths. "Who's going with me?"

Included among the surprised guests that night were: Jorge, my friend since childhood, Nelson, Enrique, Renee, Gustavo, Amelio, and my sister Margarita, two years younger than me. Olga was invited but she had to care for her ailing mother. I was nervous as I spoke because I knew my bold statement could land me in jail if anyone at the party told the authorities. Speaking out against Cuba and its government was a crime responsible for filling the country's jails with so-called dissidents from the previous three decades. Several of my classmates decided to study their shoes as the clock ticked on for what seemed like a full minute.

"Have you been drinking, Miriam?" Nelson asked, laughing and toasting me with his beer. I closed my eyes and shook my head slowly.

"No, I have not," I said. "I am dead serious." There was another silence with smiles and shuffling of the feet. Two of the guys decided about that time to walk over and study the particular type of leaves on our bushes.

"I'm with you, Miriam," Jorge said, raising his bottle and stepping up on the deck next to me. "This place is a dead end and always will be as long as Castro lives. There are no jobs and no good life for us here. Besides, I'm no good at checkers." Nobody laughed.

Sensing that their two friends were being a bit reckless, but knowing we all needed to forget our troubles for a few hours, all hands raised a bottle in the air and wished the two of us good luck. Some attendees told me later they sensed something special was going to happen that night. For one thing, they said I was not drinking and I kept busy with the food and didn't look any of them in the eyes. The party in my grandparents' back yard ended when the beer ran out and everyone went home without another mention of my announcement.

I walked the city alone the next day and thought about what I was to make of my life. Jorge and I could not pull off my plan. Had I misread my friends? I walked past the park where the old men sat. They used to be my age, I thought. Were they okay? Were my friends okay with no life of their own on this oppressive island? Maybe I should try to find others outside my circle of friends.

Two days later Nelson came by the house. "You were serious, weren't you?" he asked.

"Yes, I was serious. I am going to find a way to leave," I said, sitting on the edge of the front porch. "I am very discouraged about this country and what it can offer to young people like us. It's been this way since long before we were babies and I think it's not going to get better for a long time. I'm mad enough that I have decided to escape and I thought you'd be angry enough to join me."

"Miriam, I'm mad enough but frankly, the other night, I was afraid of a leak to the police," Nelson said. "I certainly don't want to spend 20 years in prison for treason. But now I have thought it over and I'm ready to take the chance to escape. I'm in."

"Great, Nelson," I said, giving him a hug. "Nelson, you were the smartest guy in our class and I need you with me." He was also a natural leader with movie looks so he would be helpful in recruiting others.

"I am planning to build a boat in my back yard. I need at least seven people, six to row and one to guide with a compass."

"Jorge and I will talk to the others," Nelson said. "If we can get seven or eight I'm going with you."

The following week Nelson told me all 20 of our classmates and friends from the dinner in Lu's back yard were committed to escaping from Cuba. I asked Nelson to have all of them come by at seven the following evening.

Addressing the group assembled in Lu's back yard, I had them hold up their hands to swear to secrecy. Not a word was to be said to anyone – relative, friend – no one. I gave out the assignments: Enrique, whose father was a vehicle mechanic, was to obtain six good tire inner tubes, not an easy task in Castro's Cuba. Gustavo and Angel were assigned to get the wood; Jorge, the compass; Amelio, six oars; Nelson, the Styrofoam; Renee the glue and Jose the chapapote (black tar). The materials were to be bought at various stores and junk yards to avoid suspicion and assembled in Lu's back yard in one month. Lu and the family living in the house agreed to keep everyone out of the back yard. I got a brown tarp to cover the materials when work wasn't in progress.

In early December 1990, all of the supplies were piled up under a white tarp in Lu's back yard. Two of the engineers had gone down to the docks and sketched several boats for reference in making a rough design for our boat. Jorge directed two of the others to bring specific materials to the three guys waiting with hammers. They wrapped the planks around the bulkheads that had been built for the front, middle and back of the boat. Thin plywood was used to create an inner wall and the gap between the walls was filled with Styrofoam sheets. Renee applied glue to each board as it was slipped into place. Several days were wasted tearing apart the incorrect work of the previous day.

Finally, the boat was finished and we turned it over so Renee could apply two coats of black chapapote. The boat was righted and the six inner tubes were tied on as well as rope loops for the oars. Four weeks after construction started the 22-foot-long wooden boat was declared ready. A wooden bench had been built all along the inside of the boat for passengers. It had been built by young men who had never built anything before, and it was to hold 21 nervous sailors who had never before been beyond the sandy beaches of Havana.

There was one other crucial assignment that would determine whether the risk at sea could be undertaken. Margarita had a boyfriend named Ricky who worked for the Cuban Coast Guard. My sister was a pretty girl with big brown eyes and long, wavy, light brown hair. Ricky was crazy about her. She was so-so over him but I wanted her to hold off on expressing her opinion for a while. Ricky's squad manned a patrol boat that guarded a section of the seas off the Havana coast looking for escapees trying to run for America. The coast guardsman was dedicated to his job but I could tell he was also committed to the pursuit of my sister. I sensed he might be willing to make some concession in his duties to win favor with Margarita.

Margarita and I met Ricky for lunch just after Christmas. We talked of the lack of work in Cuba and the government's failure to create jobs. Ricky was more interested in Margarita than our conversation but he seemed a little sympathetic. He was the only one at the table with a job. I decided to take a big chance and tell Ricky of my plan to escape. I didn't mention who might be going with me. He was silent for a few moments, looking at me and then at Margarita.

"Is Margarita going?" he asked, looking at me.

"No, she will stay and take care of our grandparents," I said.

Ricky drained his coffee cup and was quiet for a moment. Then, without smiling he looked at Margarita and nodded his agreement to help with the plan. I was so excited and nervous that I spilled my coffee and said we'd have to go. I shook hands with Ricky and Margarita gave him a brief kiss.

Walking home Margarita and I worried that he might change his mind and turn us in to the authorities but we had no choice. It was now or never, and never wasn't a satisfactory plan. My sister was to let me know the nights Ricky was scheduled to work so I could plan accordingly.

Two days later, Uncle Carlos backed his truck into Lu's driveway and four of the boys loaded the heavy wooden boat into the covered truck. The boys rode in the back with the boat and I directed Carlos where to go. We took the boat to a small alcove where we planned to depart. However, when the truck arrived at the beach I was surprised to see a small mob of friends and relatives who had come to say goodbye. Instead of quietly slipping the boat along the sand and into the sea, everyone leaving Cuba had a group of relatives waiting for a hug and a last kiss before they departed.

The group gathered around a small fire to pay homage to "Yemaya," the deity who is the essence of motherhood and the protector of children. Some brought the blue and white deity's favorite offerings of melons and melaco (sugar cane syrup). I looked up toward the streets along the shore hoping the police wouldn't drive by on patrol. We all held hands and prayed for the safe delivery of the little tar-covered boat to America. Finally we stepped up into the boat and a group of men ran into the surf, pushing us into the water heading north. We struggled for some time to find a rhythm to the rowing and pass the draw of the shore waves. The fire on the beach was visible for a long time and we waved long after they could see us in the dark. We could hear them singing and shouting good wishes for quite a while and then we were gone, alone, into the quiet black of the night.

I had the best view of the fading lights of Havana as I sat in the bow of the boat looking backwards over the boys-to-men of the crew. I held tight to the compass with my face inches away to read it in the dark. Finally, we were beyond the shore waves and the crew settled into a nervous awareness of the task ahead. When the last of the lights disappeared, the night seemed to close in above us and became as frightening as the black water below us. Having no way of judging whether we were making progress toward the 12-mile limit to Cuban sovereignty, the oarsmen rowed until exhaustion then switched, one-by-one with the others.

Then suddenly, somewhere in the distance, there was a sound of a boat approaching. A power boat, far off to the east at first, seemed to be heading straight toward us as the sound of the engine got louder and louder. We bent over toward the center of the boat to hide our faces. To be caught within the 12-mile limit meant arrest and imprisonment for many years. The six oarsmen moved swiftly with care not to create large splashes. Just as it seemed the roar of the motor would bring the boat into sight, the sound changed telling us the boat had mercifully turned south toward shore. I said a quiet prayer to Margarita and Ricky.

The greatest danger in the boat was that the guys would flip us as they moved side to side exchanging rowing positions. My job was to shout corrections in course when the boat veered from North. We tried not to think of the many things that could go wrong. The sea was calm with one- to two-foot waves, but waves as low as four feet could flip us into the black water.

Some who weren't tied up rowing held a picture of Yemaya tightly in both hands. They worked the oars for hours as I made sure we followed a little black hand on the compass. If we missed Key West on the west side we would never make it to the next piece of land. Would we disappear into fish food and never be heard from by our families?

In the quiet of the night, I heard a couple of whispers about the fragile nature of our plan. It didn't worry me too much as I'd read that Columbus had a few minor mutinies onboard his ships during his first crossing. I tried to divert my attention from such thoughts but I wondered if some of the men hated me. I was sure some of the families didn't agree with the crazy risk their loved ones were taking. I knew the families back home would have to go through a series of interviews by the officials but I hoped the ramifications would be limited to a one-person reduction in the familys' food rations.

"I'm going to get an automobile in America," I said. I laughed but there was no response. The only sounds were of the oars straining in their ropes before emerging with a spraying wing of water from the sea.

A small amount of water started seeping into the rear of the boat. Those sitting at the back placed their feet on their jackets to minimize the leaks and took turns ringing the water out over the side. The inner tubes and Styrofoam would have to keep us afloat if the tar failed completely.

"Damn, something just bit my toe," I shouted, surprised. "Man, it's bleeding." I had been dangling one foot off the front of the boat into the water.

"That's great, Miriam" Jorge said. "Blood in the water will draw sharks and they'll ram the boat."

"I need a rag or something to wrap my foot," I said.

"Don't get blood all over the cracker tin," Nelson said. We had our birth certificates in an old soda cracker can I had under my seat.

"I got some tar on my foot and I was trying wash it off."

"Quiet," Amelio said. "I hear something." For the second time that night we could hear a motor approaching from some distance. It got closer as we all looked toward the northeast. In the first morning light we could see the outline of a helicopter high in the sky. The chopper passed over giving no sign we had been seen.

The rowing task was proving to be harder than expected and there were complaints of calluses and cramps. The boys were the only power we had, the only chance of moving forward. They were becoming more and more exhausted, progressively slowing down on the oars. It was about this time that I thought we could have used a training routine for the boys. Those who weren't rowing tried to sleep leaning against each other. We were out of water and the boys were nearly out of power.

The sun poked an edge over the horizon giving us a lift and there was a lighter tone in the boat.

"No land yet," Jorge said standing in the middle of the boat.

"Sit down Jorge before you fall out of the boat. Let somebody taller take a look," Nelson said. "Amilio, you're the tallest. Stand up and tell us what you see.

"I see no Florida Keys in site yet," Amilio said standing. "Maybe in a few more minutes I'll look again."

The monotonous rhythm of the rowing continued as the sun streamed through a thin layer of clouds on the horizon. A few minutes later Jorge's snoring seemed in sync with the oars.

The sound of a distant power boat broke the serenade. Off to the east the motor seemed to be getting progressively louder. Had the compass corroded with salt water and failed us? Had I read the wrong end of the black hand in the dark? Did we somehow circle back to Cuban waters? Finally, we could see a boat approaching. It appeared to be a big white boat, the kind used by the Cuban Coast Guard. Getting closer it turned slightly and we were relieved to see it was an American Coast Guard boat three times as long and four times as high as our craft. Those on deck waved and we waved frantically. We had not thought much about our first contact with the Americans and none of us knew what to expect.

The boat came closer and pulled alongside, nearly swamping us in its wake. The larger boat was big enough to block the sun.

"Hello," said a tall officer in sunglasses. "Is anybody injured or sick?"

Most of us understood very little English. Nelson and I had practiced saying, "We are from Cuba. Can you help us, please?" but we both forgot the phrase completely in our exhausted and thrilled state of mind. Finally, I said, "Help," the only word I could remember. The officer switched languages.

"Sorry. Are you okay?" he asked in Spanish, looking down from the deck. We must have been a sorry sight, soaking wet, windblown, sweaty and exhausted beyond all limits.

"Yes, we are okay," I said, craning my neck and shading my eyes as I looked up into the sunlight. I tried but failed an attempt to put my bandana back over my disheveled hair which was blowing across my face.

"How many of you are in the boat?"

"Twenty one," I said.

"How many did you have when you started?"

"The same."

"Good. We're going to throw a ladder over the side," the officer said. "Climb the ladder."

Ramirez and Nelson nearly fell out of the boat trying to grab the rope ladder. The two boats bobbed in the waves, ours more than theirs, as a breeze picked up. We bumped the rescue boat hard, leaving streaks of black tar on the white hull. Not a good way to make new friends, I thought. My fellow escapees held the ladder and I was the first to climb. Nerves caused me to miss a step and nearly fall in the water. I must admit I was crying, half from fright of what was going to happen to us and half from the thrill of making it to what I hoped would be a better place. As I reached the top of the ladder I stepped with one foot onto the boat and the officer removed his hat, offered his hand and said the most wonderful words I had ever heard.

"You have reached American waters," the officer said. "Welcome to the United States of America."

Author's Note: This true story of Miriam Serrano's journey to freedom is based on her recollection of the events leading up to and during the dramatic crossing of the 90-mile stretch of ocean between Havana and the Florida Keys in January 1991. By 1996 the U.S. laws had changed requiring immigrants to actually touch land to avoid being sent back to Cuba. Miriam and the twenty immigrants she led to freedom that precarious night would have been sent back to Castro's jails if the attempt had been made five years later. Miriam and her husband, Amelio now live and work in Naples, Florida. Miriam stays in contact with Margarita, still in Cuba, as well as her former classmates now making their lives in America.

Publishing Note: The story of Miriam's Miracle was selected for publication in the Spring-Summer 2010 edition of the magazine, the MacGuffin. It was also awarded the Highly Commended Award in the Tom Howard Short Story Contest in September 2010.

Jonah Whittaker
A Short, Short Story

By Steven R. Roberts

Leaning back for a sip of coffee, his eyes landed on the wall in front of his desk. Three months ago there had been a picture of his wife, Sara, and her two teenage sons tacked into the corkboard. It was blank except for a calendar of the next two years. Jonah couldn't think about the future.

The divorce left its stingers in both parties. Jonah had searched well into his 33rd year for someone who thought he might be worthy of sharing life's journey. He had tried dating services, bars and churches but nothing happened. In the first place he wasn't any good at the small talk that seemed to be such a big part of a woman's daily need. Then there was a more important issue, at least in his mind, "heightism." The average woman's height between 30 and 40 years old was 5'4" with only 5 % of women at or below his height of 5'1". That made the population Jonah had to try to impress quite limited.

Of course he owned a mirror so he knew height wasn't exactly the only issue in attracting the opposite sex. He was going to be forty in seven months and he had to admit he wasn't particular about keeping in shape. There had been a little problem seeing his belt for the last couple of years. Yes, his hair was a fluffy brown, sort of a windblown look, and he'd been told he wore his pants to long. He reminded the office mate that mentioned it that the store bought slacks didn't come in his size and he was not about to go to a tailor for all of his clothes.

The morning after the judge made the divorce final, Jonah shook his umbrella closed and walked to the back of the Starbucks line. He looked up at the 15-year-old clerk and ordered a small black coffee and mini bran muffin. Leaving by the side door he headed his umbrella into the wind and rain for the two-block walk to the office.

"Oh, thank God, Mr. Whittaker, thanks," the new girl from the office said flashing a toothy smile and ducking under Jonah's umbrella. Folding the wet magazine she had been holding over her head. She reached down and put one hand on the umbrella stem. Jonah stretched to hold the umbrella higher and lengthened his gait.

"Morning," he said. "Not sure how much good this thing can do with the rain coming sideways." Jonah smiled, not remembering her name but recognizing her sky blue eyes and fake eyelashes. The girl was a dishwater blonde in her mid-twenties and this morning the rain was plastering wet curls against her cheeks. Jonah's normally awkward attempt at banter with a woman ran out of words earlier than usual when he couldn't even remember her name. At 5'2", including the extra thick soles in his shoes, Jonah struggled to look casual without poking her in the face with the umbrella rods. They reached the Dayton City Building but not before the rain soaked Jonah from the waist down and his companion down from the hem of her above-the-knee flared white skirt. Looking straight ahead at the lights on the elevator buttons, Jonah was sure her legs were glowing wet but he knew he wouldn't get away with a glance. When Jonah turned to let another passenger into the elevator, his cheeks turned red as his nose came nose-to-nose with Miss Whatshername. Whatever her name was, did she really need to wear high heels? In a dripping silence they rode to the fifth floor with four other workers.

Jonah trailed water into the accounting office and down the aisle to his cubicle. The cubical walls at 6' were designed to let in ambient light even for those without a window. Linda, Linda Rummy, or something like that (he suddenly remembered her name too late to use it) would be able to look over the walls and see how the weather progressed during the day. Jonah had to stand on his desk to check the weather. He removed his rubbers and set them on a small mat in the corner. Jonah set his opened umbrella in the aisle to dry and reached up to hang his heavy suit coat on a hanger looped over the wall before climbing up on his desk chair. Opening his sack from Starbucks, Jonah began his workday. Wet shoes, socks and pants would provide the office with a locker room ambience the rest of the day.

It had been six years since the city administration desk forwarded a call from an irate taxpayer. Her name was Sara Dealio and, according to her, she had been overcharged by $400 for her water bill. Jonah could tell she was quite frustrated from being transferred around so he checked it out while she was on the line. After a review of her account, Jonah advised Mrs. Dealio that the bill was correct and was the result of earlier incorrect estimated water usage. Jonah spent several minutes on the phone trying to explain the problem but the woman still didn't believe the bill was fair. She was a single mom raising two teenage boys on a teacher's salary and she didn't have $400 lying around for the water bill. Jonah agreed to personally visit the house and verify the operation of the meter. Over coffee in her kitchen he explained the bill and gave her a $50 goodwill discount.

Sara was grateful and asked him for dinner the next week. That's when he met her boys, 13 and 14. Jonah shook hands with the boys, both about his height. Jonah called the next week and they dined out, followed by a bike ride down by the lake. She was a teacher, three years younger than Jonah and a slender, statuesque 5'7". Her wispy brown hair flipped just below her ears. Jonah liked her brown eyes and the way her mouth curled upward when she spoke. Sara was a straight talker particularly when it came to her goals for the two boys. At their wedding six months later, a smiling Jonah stood at the altar beside his bride looking as if his head had been pushed down one click into his shoulders removing any signs of a neck. They had a weekend honeymoon on a train trip to see the Cleveland Browns lose 34 to 6. Jonah exhaled; he was finally out of the searching rat race. He was finally married and he had inherited an instant family.

He moved in with Sara and the boys and worked at adjusting to the role of husband and stepfather. Sara was a strict disciplinarian with the boys, listing daily tasks on the refrigerator and setting school homework rules and curfew times. Jonah had lived almost two decades on his own, however, and apparently he had picked up some less than tidy habits.

"Jonah, honey, I'd appreciate it you didn't leave your shoes by your chair when you go to bed," Sara said. What harm his little shoes might do in the den over night was a mystery to Jonah. Might a burglar trip over them while burglaring?

In addition, using a towel each morning for a week or until it turned black was supposedly repugnant, stacking newspapers on the coffee table all week was unacceptable, and using the same coffee cup every day was said to be disgusting.

Sara said she had planned on getting some help with the boys and in Jonah's mind he was trying to be helpful. According to a conversation Jonah overheard of Sara talking on the phone to a friend, she just got another boy to pick up after. To make matters worse the boys saw their new stepdad's role as being similar to a substitute teacher at school; a fresh opportunity to bend the rules during the absence of their mother. When Jonah was in charge of the house, the boys snuck out regularly for rendezvous with their friends at local burger joints, ice cream parlors and down by the river.

The real problems started when they got caught along with a friend running out of a 7-Eleven without paying for a couple of handfuls of candy bars. A large police officer brought the boys home and let them off with a lecture. Jonah hoped to win their affection by telling them he wasn't going to mention the incident to their mother. When Sara found out later she was madder at Jonah than the boys.

In a half-funk, Jonah pushed papers around on his desk all morning. At lunchtime he walked a block to the park and dried off a bench before opening his lunch sack. The rain had stopped and the sun was peeking through the partly cloudy wool sky. He opened his plain brown-wrapped copy of *Gravitas.* It was a little-known niche magazine dedicated to short people's issues in a world 8 to 12 inches taller than its subscribers. Jonah looked forward to the magazine's arrival each month for the articles and items offered. He was wearing the black enhanced-height shoes with a one-inch extra insole purchased through the magazine.

Jonah leaned forward with his elbows on his knees and slowly munched on the ham and mustard sandwich he had packed for himself. His usual Granny Smith apple and Diet Dr. Pepper would be consumed in tandem as they had been for a thousand brown-bag lunches. Jonah had lost the battle to fight off any of the 142 pounds that had taken up residence on his diminutive frame. A pound here and there added each year made a man his size seem to be nearly round.

This quarter's issue of *Gravitas* had an article listing career advice to its vertically-challenged readers:

- Try careers in radio, bus driving, telephonic marketing or software/web site development
- Stay seated when someone enters your office
- Arrive at meetings early and crank up your chair
- Meet by conference call and internet wherever possible

In sports, *Gravitas* frequently suggested fishing, hunting and horseback riding. There was another article reporting on a survey of the Fortune 500 CEOs, saying 3% were less than 5'7" in height. Jonah wondered if there were any his height. Even Ross Perot, the magazine reported, who was the brunt of short-person jokes on the late night TV shows during his campaigns for President in 1992 and 1996, was 5'7". The same article said only two of the last 12 Presidents were shorter than their opponents and only eight of 32 recent Senate races had gone to the shorter candidate. America, the *Gravitas* article concluded, is obsessed with height.

On page 58 Jonah noticed an ad that had been in the last two editions. A U.S. company was teaming up with a German chemical firm to run tests on an experimental growth-enhancing compound called "Gro-u2." Participants wanting to be considered needed to apply and be no more that 5'2", less than 30 years old and in good health. They had to sign a contract to waive litigation against the firms, commit to completing the treatments, and keep test information confidential.

"He's ready for you now, Jonah," Grace said, as she stuck her head into the cubicle at 2:15 that afternoon.

Jonah put on his damp suit coat, grabbed a pad of paper and hurried to the corner office to meet the new manager of the Accounts Payable department.

"Hi Jonah, come on in," Jonah's new boss said, motioning toward the chairs opposite his desk. Peppson T. "Pepper" Pike was a West Point graduate and a veteran of civil service jobs, that is, if you can be a career veteran after working only five years for the city. He had been a supervisor in purchasing for the previous three years, having started in the city's library systems office. Pepper served four years as an officer in the Army, including a stretch in Viet Nam, before joining the city's workforce. He was a trim 6'2" with smooth doctor-like dark brown hair and crinkly brown eyes. Pepper crushed Jonah's right hand in a handshake as they exchanged greetings. For the next ten minutes the new boss outlined his vision for Accounts Payable. Then the meeting was over.

Later, Jonah sat at his desk staring at the calendar on his corkboard wall and tapping his feet on the footstool under his desk. He had just experienced a second similarly-discouraging meeting with a new boss, having met John Dugan under the same circumstances two years earlier. It was clearly height discrimination that kept him from rising to the level of department manager. Jonah was convinced he knew more about accounts payable in a minute than Pepper or John knew all day. Oh, the system had an answer to his repeated questions regarding his promotability. In a meeting with Personnel after John's promotion, Jonah was told he was "too ponderous, too anal" to be promoted. The previous year's review had mentioned that he "lacked a sense of teamwork" in completing large projects. Another year's review said he "needed to be more innovative in solving problems."

Let's face it, he thought, staring into an open desk drawer without seeing its contents, I'm at a dead end in my never-really-got-off-the-ground career. He felt terribly used. He thought about just taking off into the woods and living off the land. At least he'd get the satisfaction of accomplishment from hunting and fishing for his supper, and a gun and fishing rod didn't pay any attention to a person's height. Maybe he'd figure out a way to buy a horse. There had been no mention in any of the performance reviews of the two incredibly complex internal projects he'd completed single-handedly when others wouldn't cooperate. There was likewise no note of his perfect record on attendance; with the exception of the week he got his gall bladder removed three years earlier. If he was a swearing man he would have leaned back in his chair and made a megaphone with his hands, letting loose with a smooth "buula sheee-it-aa" at the top of his lungs.

It seemed the city couldn't visualize a vertically-challenged man heading up a department. How could it get more pitiful than this, he thought. He had always treated people based on their values, their intellect, their character, however, it seemed the city put more emphasis on how high ones brain rode through the air each day rather than what was in it. His fingers closed on a yellow pencil in his desk drawer and he raised it slowly in the air before stabbing it down hard into a folder on his desk. The point pierced the Library Construction file and the first six documents inside before splintering across the desk. With the broken stub of the pencil still in his fist, Jonah walked out of the office leaving his coat to dry and walked to his second floor apartment.

He sat down in the kitchen and pounded his fists into the table. Lying about his age, he filled out the application for the experimental "Gro-u2" program, taking care not to let any tears stain the application.

The idea was stupid and he knew that but what the hell maybe he could get a half inch out of it. It was as dumb as a lifetime 280 pound man sending for a pill that would solve his problem.

A week later a 12-page booklet of instructions was received in German along with two bottles of large green and yellow capsules. Best he could determine by guessing and the use of a German-to-English tourist guide, the program called for test participants to take one of each pill every five days along with several glasses of a green tea concentrate and a tablespoon of a cherry extract. He couldn't read the rest of the pages but that appeared to be the essence of the test instructions. That night Jonah took one of each of the pills and the rest of the ingredients before going to bed. He was disappointed the next morning to find nothing had changed except that he was a bit too nauseated to have his standard coffee and mini muffin to start the day. He went to work as usual and functioned as usual. At lunch he could only face half of his sandwich before he threw the rest of the bag in the trash. He managed to feel better by the end of the day.

A week later there were still no results. Jonah started to feel duped and, as a last attempt, he took a double batch of pills, tea and the extract. Could he have been put in the placebo half of the test? He was barely able to focus on his work the next day in between trips to make donations at the toilet bowl.

Jonah stopped on the way home to buy a pair of slacks at Sears . He tried on his tried and true size and they didn't fit. To Jonah's surprise, he ended up with a size an inch longer and an inch smaller in the waist. Later that day a cheerful e-mail report to the test doctors indicated that test patient #23611 had grown ¾" over the first two weeks of the test. The doctors in Germany replied asking Jonah to complete a survey of his daily activities, send the results of a blood test and submit a report on the items consumed and expelled daily. His continuing nausea caused him to beg off saying he would be out of town on business for a week and he would send the reports the following week.

Three nights later he took two of each of the pills, drank three glasses of the green tea concentrate and doubled the amount of extract. The short-term result was that he had to get up to puke three times during the night.

The following week at work Homer Beam, in the next cubicle, mentioned that Jonah looked like he was losing weight. Jonah had also thought the face in the mirror looked thinner. Jonah noticed he could see his socks when he walked and assumed the new slacks had shrunk. Jonah went to the washroom and acted as if he was peeing and washing his hands three times waiting for the room to clear. Finally alone, he used a tape measure and marked the wall from 5-feet to 6-feet in one-inch increments. He quickly took off his shoes and his hand was shaking as he ran it across the wavy thin hair on top of his head.

Just then the restroom door slammed open and Pepper Pike walked in to take a pee. Jonah attempted small talk and acted as if he was getting stones out of his shoes until Pepper left the room. Jonah wasn't sure what the boss thought he was doing in the restroom. He backed against the wall again and his hand slid over the top of his head again and landed at the 5'3" mark. Jonah held his hand at the mark on the wall for a while trying to take in what had happened. He had grown 2" in two months. He repeated the fact to himself and backed into the wall again with the same result. Jonah slipped on his shoes and his eyes filled with tears as he closed the door on the third stall and happily sobbed into the toilet. His spine tingled. "My God," he said, his voice cracking into a loud whisper, "it's working." The hushed words circled the empty room in a chilling echo.

After another month of double doses, he e-mailed the German doctors that he had gained two more inches. He was nearly out of pills but he couldn't ask for a new supply because he was supposed to have a sufficient quantity to cover the next three months. He went home and lay down to contemplate living at his new height of 5'5", which he had confirmed that morning. A month earlier he would have killed for his new height but now it seemed he had come so close to his dream and fallen short. He would take the next day off work to buy new clothes and drive by Sara's work to see if they could have lunch. He couldn't wait to see her surprise at the new man who used to be her husband. Then he rethought the idea and didn't call or drive by.

About 3 pm the Germans sent Jonah an alarming e-mail.

Test Patient 23611,
You will stop test immediately due to some mixed results.
Actually, one test patient has deceased for unspecified reasons and another cannot speak due to a paralyzing stroke.
If you experience any adverse symptoms see your doctor.
All other test patients except three are receiving placebos.
Gro-u2 Test Team

Jonah read the notice over several times. The "except three" words banged around into the walls of his brain. There had only been three patients on the drugs? He placed the remaining drugs in the freezer and shivered. For the next few days he watched for any unusual symptoms, a cough, a sneeze, watery eyes, everything seemed to indicate the end was near.

The following week Jonah started waking up choking and dry heaving. Coughing and blinded by the heaves, he banged his head on the shower curtain rod so hard it knocked the rod and curtain set into the tub and he fell in after it. That's when he noticed he could no longer see the top of his head in the mirror. Instead, Jonah saw signs of a neck breaking out above his shirt collar and his nose no longer seemed to be crowding his upper lip. Without taking time to brush his teeth, Jonah hurried to the kitchen where he had marked the wall. He could smell his pits and bad breath as he slid his hand through his hair until it landed on the 5'8" mark on the doorway to the kitchen. He had grown three more inches in less than a month. Sitting in his leather chair in the living room, he worried as to what to do. This was definitely worth a few pukes but his biggest worry was that the process would all reverse one the medication ran out. He decided it was too early to buy new clothes.

Returning to work the next day, Linda gave him a wink over the cubicle walls and people kept stopping by his cubicle just to say hello. He knew they were just snooping to see if he had grown overnight. Jonah smiled. At least the jokes had turned away from the longstanding "Jonah and the mini-whale" comments he had endured all through grade school and the "fireplug" nickname his former stepsons had used for him when they thought he couldn't hear.

Two months later, Jonah had grown to the point that he had no clothes to go to work. He called in for a week's vacation. He had to return to work the coming Monday so went to a tailor and got measured for a new suit to fit his 5'10" frame, his longed-for dream height. He was now officially tall, standing one inch over the mean male height of 5'9" in the U.S."

"Linda," he shouted louder than he had intended. "Good morning, have you been keeping the place running while I've been gone?"

"Mr. Whittaker?" Linda said, flashing a toothy smile. "New suit and a new haircut, I see. You must be getting ready for a job interview."

He nodded and returned her smile.

"You can tell me, Jonah," she said, giving Jonah a gentle hip bump as they went through the doors to the building. "Where you going?"

"Never can tell, Linda," Jonah said, squinting in an effort to create a twinkle in his eyes. "Maybe I'll run for City Council. The paper says the council is hungry for leadership." Jonah walked briskly down the hall to Accounts Payable and entered his office. Exhausted from the exchange with Linda, he collapsed in his chair. His desk was covered with phone messages, all but one from known contacts. Impulsively, he dialed the odd number with a New York City area code.

"Yes," came the crisp answer.

"This is Jonah Whittaker returning your call," Jonah said.

"Yes, Mr. Whittaker, we need to talk to you about your recent participation in an illegal medical test based in Germany. You are in such a test, Mr. Whittaker? Is that correct?"

"No, I'm doing no such thing. Who is this?"

"Let's just say, Mr. Whittaker, that I represent a foreign sovereign who is most interested in your test results."

"There have been no results," Jonah said, aware he was sounding defensive. "I was in the placebo part of a test earlier this year, that's all."

"Mr. Whittaker, we have had you under surveillance for the past two months. Our agents have recorded a notable change in your appearance. My party is most interested in finding out the doses, frequencies and side effects of the medication you are taking and in recording your exact height changes. It is most important that we receive firsthand knowledge of these things as my party cannot tolerate side effects. In addition, Mr. Whittaker, we would like for you to turn over the two remaining month's supply of medications you are still holding."

"I've had no side effects and I have no pills," Jonah said, looking for a way to end the conversation. A bead of sweat let loose near the top of his spine and started the trip down the bumpy valley of his back causing him to shutter.

"In that case, Mr. Whittaker, I will need to meet with you to explain my party's interest in your test results and your remaining pill supply. We will meet soon." The heavily-accented voice hung up.

Jonah hurried out of his cubicle and down the hall to the drinking fountain to distance himself from the phone. What the hell was that guy talking about? He hadn't thought about the test being illegal and how did anyone outside the test know about it?

"How's the weather up there?" Linda asked as Jonah straightened up from the drinking fountain.

Jonah smiled and winked, turning back to his office. He sat at his desk and searched the Internet for height tests and sponsors. There were no references to recent tests in Germany or the U.S. On the first page of the search regarding height, a related news story caught his eye. Two North Koreans had been caught the previous week breaking into a German chemical company's offices. The firm wasn't operating at the time as the German government had shut them down and locked the plant a week earlier for conducting illegal chemical growth experiments. The North Korean government demanded the release of the bungling burglars.

Jonah stared at the Wikipedia bio on Kim Jong LI and read two other recent articles on the North Korean dictator. Portions of the stories looked like they could have been written about Jonah himself. "At a height of 5'3", the article said, Kim Jong LI uses elevated shoes and is obsessed with his height. The North Korean leader it was reported insisted on photo sessions with other world leaders be conducted in the sitting position. It was reported that he even invented an absurd hairstyle, which gives him two more inches in height. Jonah rocked back in his chair and took a deep breath. He wasn't good at recognizing accents but he guessed he'd heard a North Korean version of English on the earlier phone call.

Leaving for the day, Jonah scanned the parking lot to see if he was being observed. He thought he saw North Korean thugs sitting everywhere in the shadows of cars in the lot. Later, at home, he checked the front door lock twice before he went to bed.

Another week went by and Jonah measured himself at 5'11." This had happened despite the fact that he hadn't had any of the pills during that time. Reporting for work, he noticed he was able to glance over the partition to the bright sunny day outside. He returned a wave from Linda who was three or four cubicles down the maze. He smiled and decided he would ask her for lunch sometime soon. She smiled back. Looking down as he hung up his coat he saw it. On his desk was a yellow envelope with a small yellow note inside.

Mr. Whittaker,
"Go to park at 10am, to bench where eat lunch. Be alone."
Interested Party

Jonah sat down and placed his hands flat on the desk on both sides of the note. He couldn't very well go to the police or he could end up in jail. He certainly didn't want Pepper Pike to know about his scary personal predicament. It never did any good to let your personal problems spill over into the workplace. Too bad his next-door office mate and friend, Homer, was a complete nerd. Really too bad but he had no choice.

"Homer, got a minute?"

"Sure Josie. What's up?"

"I need a little favor."

At 9:45 Homer, in his tweed tam and his smudged and crooked glasses, left the City County Building and walked to a coffee shop across from the park. Five minutes later Jonah walked across the street to the park and sat on his usual bench. Nothing happened. Homer drank coffee to keep from dozing off in the hot sun. On the bench across the street Jonah's face was sweating and he was fighting the urge to bolt for home.

"Look straight ahead, Mr. Whittaker. It will be safer for you to not recognize me should you be tortured by your authorities." Jonah sensed it was the same voice he had heard on the phone. He sat back slightly and his peripheral vision indicated the man was wearing sunglasses and a baseball hat with some kind of red and white logo.

"We are on a mission, Mr. Whittaker, for our country's chairman and we dare not fail. You will tell us your formula and transfer remaining pills or we have no choice as to what to do. Don't look across the street to the cafe, Mr. Whittaker. We already have plans for your friend across the street."

Jonah looked toward the outside tables at the coffee shop. Homer was gone. The man beside Jonah on the bench was small by Jonah's most recent assessment of normal height. Could Jonah throw a fist at him and pound him into the grass beside the bench? It was the first time Jonah had ever thought such thoughts. His life had been wrapped up in conciliation, compromise, appeasement, and now he was thinking suddenly of more fight than flight. A man of 5'1" naturally develops skills in these areas for finding solutions to confrontations, or he ends up with a nose that is stretched across both cheekbones.

Jonah stood suddenly, reached across the bench and grabbed the man's shirt up close to his neck. Instinctively, he pulled him up off the bench and hit him as hard as he could with a descending right fist across his lip and nose. The man's sunglasses shattered, cutting Jonah's hand, and blood spurted from the man's nose which had lost its form. The Korean cried out and fell back over the side of the bench, falling in a little mound of pinstripes onto the grass. Jonah was spinning around holding his hand tightly and trying not to yell in pain when he saw two men come out of the trees running toward him. He willed his legs to dash toward the street where he plunged into six lanes of traffic, jumping and yelling at drivers to avoid being run over. He looked back and the two men in suits were tending to the heap near the bench and looking his way.

"Did you get a good look at them?" Jonah asked Homer as he came back to his table.

"Are you kidding?" Homer asked. "I drank three cups of coffee waiting on something to happen and just as I take a pee it all comes to be."

They walked quickly through the coffee shop and left by the rear door. The next day Jonah looked around constantly on his drive and the two-block walk to work. He skipped the stop for coffee at Starbucks and remained quite nervous until he passed through the scanning station in the building lobby. Outside the building for meetings and lunch he was careful to walk and ride with at least two other people. But then it occurred to him that somehow the "interested party's" man had managed to get a note to his desk.

Jonah stopped on the way home at a gun shop he had passed for years but never had any desire to enter. He applied for a handgun permit for a S&W M629 with a rosewood grip. He got a call at the office a few days later saying the permit had been approved. He picked it up and took shooting lessons at the inside range in the back of the store. At his new height and packing heat his confidence had grown in recent weeks. He fought the feeling because he had always observed confidence and cockiness as dangerous twin sisters. By this time he had unintentionally developed a slight swagger to his walk. It wasn't so much a John Wayne as it was the walk senior high football players developed to impress girls.

He asked Linda to lunch and she accepted. She laughed and kidded him about his new look and he was able to hold his own in the conversation. Jonah asked Pepper Pike for a raise and his boss approved it, saying it had been in the pipeline for some time. Pepper also assigned him to a special task force the mayor had started to develop strategic plans for the city, a plum assignment with good management visibility.

Then there was another note that appeared after lunch one day. It gave instructions similar to the first note except the meeting was to be on the patio outside of the coffee shop. Homer was useless so Jonah went alone to the shop. He bought a coffee and brought it to the table next to the wrought iron fence along the sidewalk. A little man in sunglasses and a dark bruise on his cheek sat down at the table and stared at Jonah. "You will not send us back to our chairman empty-handed and humiliated in defeat," he said through a jaw that exposed wires when he tried to speak.

"Nice new sunglasses. I would like to help you and your friends," Jonah said, "but I don't have what you want. I am not participating in a growth test and if I was in such a test I wouldn't have a supply of extra pills left over; I'd take them. I suggest you try to find the German manufacturer and have them make some for you and your interested party. If you keep threatening me I will expose your dictator as a blackmailing thug in pursuit of a few precious inches of height to assuage his consuming ego. Then what will the world think of your little leader?"

"Mr. Whittaker, we believe you are not being truthful with us. The manufacturing plant in Germany has been burned to the ground along with the Gro-u2 formulas. We have information from one of the former employees of the company that you are the only patient who can tell us what we need to know." He paused and looked at the car parked next to the curb before saying, "You will stand now and come with us. I believe we can come to an arrangement regarding the information and the pills we must have."

The man stood and pulled a long knife from his suit pocket and slapped Jonah with it, causing a gash across his cheek. Blood sprayed over the table and Jonah's coat sleeve. "That is for you breaking my favorite sunglasses, Mr. Whittaker," he said through his teeth.

He pointed again to the car. Jonah remained seated at the table with his left hand holding his face, blood slowly oozing through his fingers.

"Now, Mr. Whittaker," the man said, "we are losing time and patience. We may not kill you unless we have to but in the end you may wish we would. If necessary, you will be taken to our camp and there we will negotiate in the name of our chairman."

Jonah stood, covering one eye and bloody cheek with his hand, and stepped slowly toward the gate to the short fence that surrounded the patio. He sensed he would not survive a ride in the car, where he could see two other men waiting. He turned slowly and looked at the man with the knife held discreetly in his hand and trailing up his sleeve. Jonah fumbled to remove the lid from the coffee with one hand and brought the cup to his lips, quickly turning and throwing the full cup of coffee into the shorter man's face. Jonah drew his pistol and slapped the shorter man hard across the cheek causing something to break inside the man's head.

"Stay in the car!" he yelled pointing his gun at the two occupants in the car.

Jonah dragged the man down the row of parked cars, leaving a streak of blood on the sidewalk. He held his gun to the man's bloody head before dropping him and jumping between cars. Jonah ran along the street side of the parked vehicles as the two men jumped from the dark car firing, with bullets smashing windshields and ricocheting off the vehicles. He turned the corner and slipped through a women's clothing store and out the back door. Jonah held his gun at the ready and ran low to the ground down the alley, turning up the street just as the two men came running around the corner. Bullets cut through the air on both sides of Jonah as pedestrians dove for cover. He jumped down behind a cab parked at the curb and returned fire. The cabbie jumped out shouting expletives in a language Jonah didn't understand and ran.

From behind the cab Jonah could see the shooter was crouched down behind a bright red Volkswagen. Where was the other guy, Jonah wondered. From across the street came the answer in the form of a burst of gunfire, shattering glass just over Jonah's head. Jonah turned and released three rounds toward the second shooter; the man in the dark suit yelled something then fell silently to the pavement. Jonah jumped in the cab, which was still idling, and pulled out into the street busy with traffic. He lay down sideways on the seat and drove quickly past the first shooter. Three bullets hit the side of the cab, removing the side window and ripping at the doors. Luckily, the tires remained in working order and the gas tank didn't explode.

In the rear view mirror Jonah could see the first shooter limping across the street to tend to the second. He made his way out to the interstate highway and drove north for two hours before exiting in search of a Target store. His shirt was bloody and his pants felt damp. He pushed the cart in front of him as he shopped. Fifteen minutes later he emerged wearing new khakis, underwear and a light blue shirt. All three were in regular sizes, those he never thought he would get a chance to buy.

Back on the highway, he drove for another hour before pulling into a café across the street from a LaQuinta hotel. He parked the cab behind the café and went in.

"Hi, I'm Kayhart," the waitress said. "Know what you want, Deary', or need a menu? Whoa Honey, you look a mess. You been pecked at by a bird and sliced up like a watermelon. Let me get something to clean up your face."

"Don't worry Miss. I'm okay, just a misunderstanding with a couple of fellows back down the road," Jonah said.

"What's your name Honey?" the waitress said returning with a warm towel and proceeded to wipe the blood off of Jonah's face.

"Jonah."

"Well isn't that just biblical?"

"Just coffee for now," Jonah said, wiping his face with the towel. What has happened to my so-called life, he thought. How did my mediocre, humdrum days get turned so upside down?

"You look like a growing boy, Deary'," Kayhart said. "How about a piece of rhubarb pie, ay? Made it myself 'bout an hour ago specially cause I knowed you was coming."

Kayhart swished back to the kitchen in her white blouse and red dress full to her ankles and returned with the pie. Jonah smiled after her. She had an interesting deep voice, he thought, with lines on her face that recorded a fun life.

"I don't recognize your accent," he said, feeling his way with the small talk.

"I've got no accent, Honey. You do," she said. "But for what it's worth I'm Canadian. I grew up on a small farm east of Windsor."

"Are you a northern wetback?" Jonah asked.

"No," she said laughing, "I came over to go to school up in Detroit at Wayne State and stayed. A few years back I became legal. I still feel out of place but I'm legal."

"I know how you feel," Jonah said."

"Well, enjoy the pie, ay," Kayhart smiled, emphasizing the ending to the sentence and walked to another table.

The pie lived up to its billing.

"Thanks for the pie," he said, standing to leave, "and for cleaning me up."

"Weren't nothing, Honey," she said. "You look better now. You come back sometime and I bake you a whole pie for yourself.

Next morning, the paper outside his door had the story of three North Koreans in a gunfight with an unknown gunman. He was relieved not to see his picture involved with the story. After coffee and a bagel from the lobby, Jonah walked into town where he bought a bus ticket to Detroit. The next morning he signed up in the hotel lobby for a shuttle that took a group of the hotel guests to the Windsor, Canada, casinos. Authorities were getting ready to require passports at the start of the new year but it hadn't happened yet.

That night Jonah walked away from the bus group and paid cash for a train ticket to Toronto. Two days later he ended up in Kitchener. Eventually he landed a part time job as a bouncer and driver for a bar named Frozen Solid. He was around 6'1" and nearly 200 pounds by now with a black beard and metal-framed glasses. The pills had run out and Jonah watched for signs that he might start shrinking. He had a real scare the night the Toronto Raptors basketball team came into the bar one night on their way to an exhibition game.

Shortly after arriving he saw an updated newspaper report of the gunfight down in the states. It reported that the three North Koreans were members of Kim Jong LI's honor guard and they were said to be in the U.S. looking for artwork and other western treasures requested by the North Korean president. The body of the man who was killed was being accompanied back to Korea by the two survivors of the gunfight. The paper also listed Jonah Whittaker as a man of interest for the police and gave his description, including a height of about 5'8". The height estimate, Jonah thought, must have been based on an adjustment to his official work records. He thought about calling the paper to correct the description. The next day Jonah, or "Jack E. Mack," as he was now known, called for his pay at the bar and left town.

The Mounties visited Kitchener twice that winter looking for Whittaker, aka Jack E. Mack, and interviewed people who knew him when he lived there. They also searched in Northern Canada but they've found no trace. The Mounties discount stories that Whittaker may somehow be tied into the "Big Foot" stories that circulate in the press each year.

Locals are tight-lipped about it but they say he was last heard of living with a former barmaid named Kayhart who was last seen at her place of employment in Sandusky, Ohio. Word is the couple lives in a small log cabin and stays busy growing vegetables, raising chickens, and riding horses along the wooded trails near Hudson Bay. They survive, so the locals say, by fishing, hunting and cutting wood. There have been no recent reports on the size of the man.

The Carpathian Cook
Fright on the Night Shift At Sea

By Steven R. Roberts

"Damn it Frankie, the sticky buns were alright last night but the captain said the pies were a waste of good apples. One more screw up and the captain is going to force me to move you to the boiler room."

"Boss, if that happens you'll have to do the cooking yourself so I think we ought to act like we're on the same side out here in the middle of this ocean.

Morris Ogden, the ship's head chef was having a brief meeting with two of his cooks, Franc Gerbec and Casper Bovich before the start of the night shift on the RMS Carpathia. The ship was mid-ocean on its trip from New York to Fiume (now Rijeka), Croatia. The date, April 14, 1912, was special and Morris wanted to make sure preparations were in order for the captain's birthday dinner the next evening.

"Remember," Morris told Casper, "the captain is partial to the salmon appetizer sliced thin and the brisket cut thick with lots of gravy."

"Frankie," Morris told his pastry chef, "the captain wants a white cake with chocolate icing and he likes the icing hard as a brick. You got that?"

"I got it boss," Franc said. "If you want two cakes just let me..."

"Wraangg, Wraangg, Wraangg," came the blast from the ship's horn. It was 12:41 in the morning.

"All hands to your emergency stations! This is a code five alert! The captain has ordered all hands to their emergency stations."

Six crew members on the night shift had been having lunch in the galley. They left their food trays on the table and hurried to their stations. Heading upstairs to meet with the captain, Morris told his two cooks to continue in the kitchen.

"What is the matter?" Franc asked.

"I don't know," Casper said. "I'm going to keep going with meal prep for tomorrow. What the hell could be so important at this hour of the morning?"

"I've actually got the cake done," Franc said, so I'll work on tomorrow's pastries.

Franc and Casper would not normally have been given spots on the crew of the single stacker passenger ship leaving Trieste, Italy. But two months earlier when the ship was ready to leave the two regular chefs' assistants were in jail. They had been drinking down at Steffi's Place over on Fortunato Piazza the previous night. They had busted up the place and got themselves arrested. Captain Rostron wasn't about to change the date of Carpathia's departure for a couple of drunks.

Early that morning, Franc Gerbec happened to be standing in the dark at the employment line near the end of Panza Piazza. He needed to earn money to pay for passage to America. Franc had no marketable skills but he was confident about his chances of finding employment. His gift for persuading people came from years of herding reluctant goats. Franc had worked on the family farm his whole life so he knew it would be difficult to find real money- making employment. His family's farm was just over the Slovenian border outside Maribor in Austria where Franc lived with his wife, Avina, their 14-year-old son, Mikhail, and his parents. Times had been tough on the farm with unwilling, rocky soil, cold winters and relatively cool summers. If that wasn't enough incentive to leave the region, it was clear that war was coming to Europe. Tensions were high and overlapping defense agreements meant it would likely take only one spark to set the whole continent ablaze. Franc and his wife had decided he would find a way to get to America where he was to earn money for passage for Avina and Mikhail.

Here in the cold morning the line of prospective workers was long and the number of jobs would undoubtedly be short.

"We need a painter," a woman's deep voice shouted from the front of the line. Three men leaped to the front, fighting over the hiring slip of paper. Franc's Italian was limited so he had no idea what she had said.

"We need a pastry cook," the broad Italian woman said in more of a gravel grunt than a statement.

"Si," Franc shouted, starting to move forward. "What did she say?" he asked one of the men he passed.

"They need a cook," the man said in Slavic.

"I am cook," Franc said.

The woman looked up and stood to see around those in the front of the line. A short man in a baggy charcoal coat was smoothing his wavy black hair as he approached the desk.

"Can you cook pastries; you know pies, cookies, breads?" the lady asked, adjusting to her native Croatian tongue. "They are looking for somebody short so you may have a chance. There's not much room to spare down there."

"Yes, I can cook all of those things," Franc lied. "I also know milk and cheese," he added more truthfully.

"Good, I hired another Slovenian earlier this morning for the Carpathia. It's a ship. You will get along fine. Here, you need to report at the end of the fifth pier on the left," the woman said, holding out the hiring slip to Franc.

"Thank you. I will go now."

"Son," the lady said, "the hiring slip says the ship is making a quick turnaround in New York and coming back." They want the new hires to stay on for two loops to America."

"That will be okay," Franc said. "I need to earn money to bring my family over." He walked to the end of the street, turned left and ran to the ship.

The next day the ship departed and was on its way down the Adriatic. Chef Morris walked Franc and the other new hire, Casper, through the ship's galley and the planned menus for the voyage. Morris had ship's recipes for some of the items but others, particularly baked goods, depended on a little of this and a pinch of that. The head chef monitored his new assistant cooks' work for the first few days then he moved on to his other duties.

"Franc, how's the guessing going so far?" Gasper asked with a laugh. The two new cooks had fallen into a supportive friendship for the voyage.

"We got it made," Franc said. "Of course, I hope the captain doesn't find out I threw the first two batches of muffins overboard this morning. The fish loved them but the first mate took one bite and spit it back in my face. My mother and my wife made it look so easy. I guess my memory is not as good as I thought. I've added more sugar and milk to this batch. Here, try one and let me know what you think. I need to get this right before they find me out."

"It tastes okay to me," Casper said. "Of course, Captain Rostron and most of the crew are British so who knows what the hell might taste good to them. I should know. I'm trying to learn how to overcook the meats we are going to serve."

On the east bound loop the Carpathia had transported passengers and members of a Canadian expeditionary force to Trieste. On the return trip the ship was carrying mostly Slavic and Italian passengers out of harm's way to England and most were heading to America. The ship proceeded west through the Mediterranean and took a wide path around the continent, hoping to avoid the German U-boats. On March 10th the Carpathia arrived in Southampton and four days later it had taken on supplies and added passengers for America. Sailing west out of the English Channel, the ship joined a caravan headed for New York. The single stacker was the slowest and the last ship in the caravan.

Carpathia's crew members were hard working people hired on to work for the voyage to America. In Franc Gerbec's case, he had planned on finding a job in America so he could make enough money to send for his wife and son. He wanted to have the family safely settled in America before war broke out in Europe. The round trip stipulation of employment for new employees was an unexpected bonus for Franc. The first, westward, crossing was to pay for his passage but he would be paid a wage for the rest of the loop.

"Frankie, I just got word that the captain and two of his officers are on their way down for coffee," Morris reported an hour after the distress signal. "Bring out some of those muffins you've been making."

"Coming up hot and sticky, Boss," Franc said.

When they arrived, the officers spoke in whispered tones and soon departed for the upper decks. The captain had ordered extra crews to feed coal to the boilers and had the steam heat to the rooms turned off. The ship vibrated to the rhythm of the straining engines, reaching a maximum speed of 17 knots.

"Did the captain say what was going on top side?" Casper asked.

"He didn't say much," Morris said. "Apparently there is another ship in trouble. We are 58 miles away and I heard we're the closest rescue ship in the area.

Several decks above the kitchen, in Carpathia's Marconi Room, the tragedy of the night had been frighteningly clear for some time.

12:25 am – First distress signal received from the ship Titanic. "Come at once we have struck a berg."

Carpathia – Do you require assistance?

Titanic – Yes, come quick.

Soon after the officers left the galley Morris reported that the new super-sized passenger ship, the RMS Titanic, had signaled that it had been "hit by an iceberg". Apparently, it was a serious accident and the Carpathia was rushing to the scene.

12:28 to 12:34 – Titanic sent messages requesting assistance and giving its position as 41.46N.50.24W.

Mount Temple, Frankfurt, La Provence, Ypiranga, Prinz Friedrich Willhelm, and Caronia responded trying to clarify the urgency of the request.

Frankfurt – What is the matter with you?

Titanic – We have struck an iceberg and sinking. Please tell Captain to come.

As the night went on, exhausted men covered in sweat and black coal dust started showing up in the crew galley. They stumbled through the food line before collapsing into the wooden benches at the tables.

"We need more water out here, Frankie," Morris shouted. "These guys need to wash the dust down so they can swallow." Franc brought cups of water and went back to bring bread. The men choked on the water and spit globs of black coal dust on the floor.

12:45 and 12:50 – Titanic – SOS sent to sister ship Olympic, 500 miles away. Titanic also sent SOS to all ships giving corrected position of 41.46 N.50.14W. – Several ships reply but Carpathia, 58 miles away, is said to be the nearest ship.

"Casper, pull ahead the meals planned for tomorrow's lunch," Morris said, sticking his head into the kitchen. "Frankie, you need to do the same. These men need energy to keep them going through the night."

"What?" Casper asked. "That's impossible. Those meals will take hours to prepare."

"You heard the boss," Franc said. "This is no time to get sent to the engine room." There was no more experimentation time for the two cooks. The rolls and buns had to be right the first time. If they weren't Franc knew he might be thrown overboard covered head to foot with sticky buns.

1:00 to 1:30 am – Carpathia and several other ships monitor messages from the Titanic and respond that they are proceeding full speed to help. Most are hundreds of miles and several hours away.

Titanic to all ships – We are in collision with berg. Sinking head down. Come as soon as possible.

Titanic to Olympic – Get your boats ready. What is your position?

Olympic – Are you steering southerly to meet us?

Titanic – We are putting women off in the boats. Women and children in boats, cannot last much longer.

The Carpathia's passengers had been jarred out of their sleep by the realization that the mighty Titanic had struck an iceberg and was in danger of sinking.

"This is nuts," a man from Manchester said. "They hit an iceberg and now we are speeding into the same trap."

Captain Rostron had electric lights hung along the sides of the ship and the gangway doors opened. He also ordered the lifeboats to be swung out over the sides of the ship.

"Forget the meals," Morris told the two cooks. "We need to bring hot drinks to the deck. Make tea and coffee and throw together some kind of soup. Frankie, bring some muffins and cookies."

"Make up your mind, Boss," Franc said. "Which is it to be, meals or drinks?"

"It's both and everything else we have in the cold locker," Morris said

"Should I cut up the captain's birthday cake?" Franc asked with a smile.

"I didn't know you had it done. Let me see it," Morris said, opening the door to the cold locker. He approached the cake and knocked on the brown crusty-hard icing. "It's perfect, Frankie, the icing is as hard as a brick. The captain will love it. Let's hold off on serving it. Now is most likely not a good time to present it to the captain."

Up in the control tower, Captain Rostron ordered blankets and warm clothing to be brought to the deck. He had nets and ropes rigged over the sides for the survivors. He also took the ironic action of having the ship's rear cargo crane ready so it could lift the survivors' luggage and mail aboard.

1:45 Titanic message picked up by Carpathia – Come as quickly as possible old man; the engine room is filling up to the boilers.

2:17 Titanic's final message – Calling All Ships (an earlier version of SOS). Titanic's signal ended abruptly and power was gone.

And so was the Titanic, Captain Rostron must have feared. No ship sunk out here in the night without taking a piece of every other captain with it. With its engines vibrating at maximum capacity, the Carpathia finally arrived at 3:30 am at the exact coordinates provided by the Titanic's final message. The ship stopped and the Carpathia's passengers and crew came out on deck to see what was left of the Titanic and the souls it carried. Instead they found an empty, eerily quiet and calm night. The realization that the ship was gone and there were no survivors caused some to hug their fellow travelers and sob. Strangely enough, there were also no dead bodies to be retrieved.

Franc and Casper stood together and peered into the darkness. The same icebergs that had sunk the Titanic were hidden in the dark, standing guard ready to take down any other ships wavering off course. Around 4 o'clock the captain stopped all engines allowing passengers and crew to strain to hear any trace of survivors. Word was that more than 2,200 passengers and crew who had departed from Southampton. They could see nothing but a tame black sky and sea.

"Don't you wonder if our captain got the coordinates wrong?" Franc whispered, balancing two trays of muffins with imbedded pieces of the last couple of bananas they had on board. He and Casper were serving coffee, soup and snacks to the hushed assembly on deck.

"I doubt it," Casper said, "He's been sailing for a long time. Maybe they got rescued by an earlier ship."

"We were the nearest," Franc said. "But if they are out there, why don't they shout or send up a signal?"

"I'd say they're all gone."

"Quiet," an officer said. "If there are survivors who haven't yet frozen to death, they are undoubtedly in shock from the cold and from shouting for hours. Listen."

"Two o'clock!" shouted one of the crew from the control tower. "There's a green flare at two o'clock."

The Carpathia sent up flares and out of the dark came a lifeboat full of frozen survivors rowing slowly toward the ship. The captain maneuvered the Carpathia to give the lifeboat leeward protection. Slowly the lifeboat came alongside the gangway door around 4:10 am and its passengers started to come on board. The first survivors confirmed that the unsinkable Titantic had indeed sunk.

The first boat was followed by a second full of sobbing and frightened survivors and then others appeared out of the night. Some of the inflatable lifeboats had partially collapsed leaving survivors clinging to parts of the boats and suffering from exhaustion and hypothermia. The Carpathia's crew worked in shifts hauling passengers aboard and wrapping them in blankets. Children were hauled aboard in mail sacks by the ship's cranes. Four hours later the last of the survivors, 705 in total, were brought aboard.

"Hot coffee and muffins," Franc said, Morris having coached him on the way to approach these new passengers. He and Casper stood near the gangway door as the frozen and confused passengers came aboard. The women looked closely at the faces of the welcoming party, desperately seeking any sign of their husbands.

"Have you seen Walter, Walter Donnellson?" a lady asked, pleading with Franc. "Have you seen him?"

"No Miss, sorry," Franc said. He raised the tray of warm muffins but the lady showed no interest. She asked other crew members and then fell sobbing in a heap against the wall. Franc put down his tray and covered her with a dry blanket.

Most would cling to the belief that their husbands were in another lifeboat or had been rescued by another vessel, a misconception that would last at least until they arrived five days later in New York. The luxury liner had started its maiden voyage with 2,228 passengers and crew and 1,523 had gone to rest deep under the frozen surface where the Carpathia stood in the dark that morning.

"Boys, we need to talk," Morris said, returning to the kitchen. "We have increased the number of warm bodied souls on this ship by about a third so we have to make some serious changes in the meals."

"I have enough food stock inventories to feed the 1,700 people of the Carpathia for the next five days," Franc said.

"Me too," Gasper said. "How many survivors did we pick up tonight?"

"I think I heard it was around 700," Morris said. "We'll need to cut back but the captain expects a high-end kitchen and I don't intend to sacrifice my reputation over this accident."

"Cut back? We'll need to cut meals," Franc said. "I'd say we need to go to two meals a day and cut portions. Cheese sandwiches, that's it, cheese sandwiches all around. Otherwise we are going to have some very mad and skinny customers before we reach New York."

"Haven't you heard the story in the Bible about 40 loaves?" Casper asked.

"Yes but I'm not sure I can repeat it out here in the middle of the Atlantic," Franc said.

"Okay, okay, I'll talk to the captain about going to two meals a day," Morris said. "I'll take him his birthday cake. Maybe that will put him in a good mood."

"Ah, wait a minute, Boss," Franc said. "In the panic last night we ran out of food for the survivors. I cut the captain's cake into small pieces and fed it to the new passengers. It was also popular on deck and, as I recall, you even had a piece."

"I don't remember eating cake last night," Morris said.

"Maybe this will remind you," Franc said. He handed the head chef a wrapped piece of cake, the one he had saved for the captain.

Ah, well done, Frankie," Morris said, smiling for the first time that night. "I'll make sure the captain enjoys his cake at afternoon tea today. In the meantime plan for two meals a day, thin down the recipes, and cut the portions to everybody. New York is five days from here."

"Did ol' Morry really have a piece of cake last night?" Casper asked when he and Franc were alone.

"No not really," Franc said smiling.

The Carpathia docked in New York amid a flurry of news reporters and anxious families. The eight new crew members were relieved of their obligation to complete the second trip across the ocean and given a choice of remaining in New York or staying with the ship for the next loop. Franc decided to stay even though he didn't have friends or family to give him a place to stay. Casper also stayed but he soon traveled to his family in Wisconsin. Two days after unexpectedly arriving back in America Franc traveled south by bus and eventually made contact with Slovenian friends in the Slavic community of New Smyrna Beach, Florida. A year later Franc was able to arrange to have his wife and son join him. Despite the horror of that night on the black sea, for all of his life Franc Gerbec retained the wonder of his journey and the miracle of living and raising his family in America.

Author's Note: My thanks go to Tom Gerbec, Naples, Florida, for relating to me the basic elements of this story about his grandfather's historic voyage to America. This is a fictionalized and dramatized version of "Gramps'" life-changing story.

The RMS Carpathia of the Cunard Steamship line was launched in 1903 and sunk off the southwest tip of England by a German U-boat in July 1918.

More Than Simply Arthritis

By Shirley Cheng

"A...ar...art..." Juliet muttered, running her finger down her red English-Chinese dictionary and stopping when it reached its destination: arthritis. She read the definition of the name the doctor had just recently labeled on her baby daughter. "Arthritis? I know many people who have it, so it does not seem so serious." Yet it seemed to be deadly on her 11-month-old infant, who was, at that moment, in the hospital undergoing test after test to validate the doctor's diagnosis.

The previous doctor to whom Juliet had taken her child told her that there was absolutely nothing wrong with her. At first, it comforted Juliet. But quickly that comfort turned into discomfort. If nothing was wrong with her daughter, then why was she screaming in agony? Why would her tiny body shake whenever she applied even the slightest pressure on her legs? And why were her joints red and swollen? No, there must be something the matter with her, and now she knew that something was arthritis. Still, arthritis, at least what she was gathering from the dictionary, paled in comparison to what the baby was going through. There must be more than simply arthritis. When test results came back, they did confirm that there was indeed more than simply arthritis--it added two more words in front of arthritis.

"Mrs. Cheng, Shirley has juvenile rheumatoid arthritis," announced the doctor.

"Is that an important change in the diagnosis?" Juliet asked.

"Yes, Mrs. Cheng, I'm afraid it is," said the doctor.

Once back home from the hospital after receiving the confirmed diagnosis, Juliet got out another one of her trusty books to consult: her Chinese medical dictionary, which listed many of the known diseases accompanied by photographs that were anything but pleasing to the eye. Juliet quickly read through the symptoms of this form of arthritis, and when she read that there was no cure, her heart--or what was left of it after days of fruitless guessing, worrying, searching--sank.

Shirley had juvenile rheumatoid arthritis. That idea further tore Juliet's heart to unrecognizable pieces. Her heart began its grinding process when Shirley developed a high fever five days after receiving a tuberculin skin test. Soon, the child cried uncontrollably whenever Juliet gently touched her left leg.

"It could cripple my pearl!" exclaimed Juliet when that possibility hit her.

However, as soon as that negative thought sprang into mind, she quickly washed it away. She salvaged the pieces and put her painful heart back together again. Let that disease try to win and fail. Then and there, she vowed: she was going to use everything she had and anything the world offered to make life the best experience for her daughter, and she would see to it that Shirley would be the prettiest princess on a wheelchair the world had ever seen. The disease could only touch her body; with Jehovah God's help Juliet would make sure it would never touch her soul. She knew she would stand strong by her daughter's side at all costs. If she had to carry her over high mountains, she would. If she had to rescue her from the depths of the oceans, she would. And if she had to send her high to reach a star or two, she would gladly. If it had to take a whole world for her to be a successful mother, then let it be so, for Shirley was more than any world to her.

Thus, in a moment it all changed. Juliet entered a brave new world alone with the aim of coming out as one team of victorious mother and daughter. Many challenges awaited her, and with every defeat of the first, she would graduate only to learn that tougher obstacles needed to be conquered.

During the initial stage of the challenges, Shirley's days were spent in constant pain, making all daily chores, like dressing and bathing, highly difficult. Nights were spent with Juliet rocking the suffering baby to sleep, often lasting long into the early morning. Juliet became physically worn down and exhausted. Twenty-four hours and seven days a week were used up for the baby, who, by her 13th month of life, was knocking on death's door. The crippling disease had rapidly spread to nearly all of the joints in Shirley's body, causing excruciating pain. She was like a statue, unable to move or sit.

Seeing that American hospitals offered no relief for Shirley, Juliet took her to China, her native country, to seek remedies that could ease Shirley's suffering, and therefore, save her from a fate worse than death. And that took Juliet to the second stage of unrelenting challenges, which consisted of six trips to China within a span of ten years.

As Juliet had fervently hoped, Shirley's life was not only saved, but she, at age four, also could experience one full year of walking after receiving Western shots combined with massage therapy. For the first time, Shirley explored a world she had never really known: the world outside of hospital walls. She was fascinated by everything she saw, heard, and touched, experiencing the new feelings that came with walking, running, and dancing. At the end of the second stage, Juliet had achieved her primary goal: stabilizing Shirley's health and keeping her happy at all times; Shirley's physical pain was considerably tamed under herbal medicines.

Juliet entered the third stage with an expanded version of that goal: to maintain Shirley's well being in mind, body, and spirit, as she pursued knowledge for the very first time. Owing to years of hospitalization between America and China, Shirley received no education until age 11. Back then, she knew only her ABCs and very little English. She knew that two plus two equals four, and three times five is fifteen; she had no idea from where rain comes or why we see a beautiful rainbow after refreshing spring showers, so she was put in a special education class in elementary school. However, being the happy and hopeful girl that Juliet had tirelessly brought her up to be, her soul was uncontaminated by depression or sadness. So it was open to freely absorb knowledge, just like crystal clear water could effortlessly flow through a mud-free river without any hindrance.

Therefore, she absorbed all that was taught in class and mostly self-taught herself how to read; like Cookie Monster, she devoured one book after another as though they were chocolate chip cookies, yet always hungered for more. Shirley's hunger for knowledge soon paid off. After only about 180 days of attendance, her special education teacher told Juliet: "She is ready to go to a regular sixth grade class and she will do very well in it." Shirley and Juliet were off to a whole new world of a different set of hurdles.

Indeed, just as Juliet had first expected at the beginning of their hardship, there was so much more than simply arthritis. There was the relief Juliet felt when her baby's life was miraculously prolonged; there was the pain that cut through her whenever Shirley cried; there was the thrill the mother-daughter team experienced when Shirley first walked; there was the heartache that stabbed Juliet when the walking days ended after the quality of the shots went downhill; there was the injustice when Juliet was charged with seven-year old child abuse and the state took away her parental rights after she refused unwanted and harmful treatments for her daughter; there was the joy when Shirley swam into the mainstream school system with a smile that spoke a thousand words; there was the pride Juliet held when Shirley scored numerous awards and high grades as a high honor student; there was the frustration when they tried to find compassion from apathetic people; and there was the laughter shared when Shirley twirled around and around in her power wheelchair in their cozy living room.

And as the years passed, there was the horror when Shirley lost her eyesight at the age of 17; but there was the immeasurable happiness when Shirley conquered her blindness to become an award-winning author with 20 book awards and a motivational speaker. Above all, there is the strong love and the inseparable bond formed between this team, cheerleaders to each other. Through their trials and tribulations, two bodies have become one spiritually, living in each other's heart, ever wishing, hoping, praying, and dreaming together.

And now, after passing who knows how many stages of exams and quizzes, with Jehovah as their Teacher, mother and daughter, hand in hand, have graduated magna cum laude, and they impatiently look forward to attending the next class together so they can discover and embrace what more may await them than simply arthritis.

Author Bio: Shirley Cheng (b. 1983) is a blind and physically-disabled award-winning author (with 20 book awards, including nine Parent to Parent Adding Wisdom Awards and Mom's Choice Awards), motivational speaker, self-empowerment expert, poet, author of nine books, contributor to 19 books, parental rights advocate and Board member of the World Positive Thinkers' Club. Visit Shirley at http://www.shirleycheng.com

"Although I'm blind, I can see far and wide; even though I'm disabled, I can climb high mountains. Let the ropes of God haul you high."

Cold Hayride

By Steven R. Roberts

My name is David Wood and I was 24 at the time of this story. Back then I was the quietly confident type, but make no mistake about it, I knew almost everything there was to know. With a youthful sense of urgency I was a subscriber to the "ready, fire, aim" club. Listening to other voices was not my strength. The day I stopped by to visit a ranch in Wyoming was a chilling reminder of the mountain of stuff I still didn't know.

The X Bar C Ranch was 40 miles northwest of Dubois, Wyoming and 9,000 feet into the eastern Rockies. The family owners of the ranch had raised hay and cattle for decades along the banks of the Wind River. The ranch supplemented its income by offering a five-day ranching adventure to city folks. On a bright and cold Saturday morning in early December, 1940, my wife Dorothy and I coaxed my old Ford up the snow-covered winding dirt road to the ranch for a one-night stay. New snow had fallen the day before and the giant pines on either side of the road formed a tunnel over the road with their snow-loaded branches. Around the 5,000-foot mark we were treated to some spectacular views of the mountains, rivers and valleys as the road wound its way along the cliffs hugging the sides of the mountains. About this time the guardrails disappeared and we had a few deeply religious "Jesus" moments as we slid around the bends of the one-lane road.

The ranch owner's sister, Mary, had invited us to stay at the X Bar C for a day as both a friendly gesture and a way to promote a longer stay at a later date. She ran the motel where we were staying that summer while I worked on the public works project building a road through the Togwatee Pass into Grand Teton and Yellowstone National Parks. As a recent engineering graduate I was glad to have a job and the project also helped pass the time while I waited on the draft board to call me into the Navy.

Fritz, the ranch operator, waved from the corral attached to the right side of a white barn as we pulled under the archway at the main gate. We came to a stop as my old reliable Ford gasped for one last breath of thin air and spit a plum colored cloud into the mountain air. I had two spare quarts of oil in the trunk for the trip back to Togwatee.

"Hi folks," Fritz shouted as he approached, wiping his leathery hands on a rag from his back pocket and stomping the snow from his boots. "Hope Mary's map wasn't too confusing. There are several cut backs and splits in the road coming up here."

Wavy salt and pepper strands of hair ran from under the rancher's sweat-stained floppy hat. His barrel chest preceded his fleece vest, open despite the temperature. Fritz had a square jaw and smiling eyes fit over a stocky build with a trace of middle-aged spread.

"We did OK," I said, shaking hands and introducing Dorothy.

"Welcome, little lady," Fritz said, helping to get Dorothy's bags out of the car.

"Never saw a print or a map I couldn't figure out," I said, more boastfully than intended. "Actually, we got lost twice," I said, trying to recover, "and my wife looked a little car sick toward the end but we made it."

"Good," Fritz said, turning toward the farmhouse. "Bring your bags and let's go in and meet Lillie. Our 5-day adventure guests stay in the bunkhouse but my wife's got you two set up for spending tonight in the house."

That morning as we were leaving the hotel, Mary had mentioned that about ten years earlier she and her brother had inherited 60 acres along the south side of the Wind River plus a 40-acre meadow about four miles up and across the river. Fritz managed the farm. Our first look at the house told us Fritz spent his maintenance money on the two barns. The porch sagged a bit on the left side and the house appeared to have survived in a gradual graying state without paint for several years. One of the brown shutters had fallen off and was lying sideways on the floor, leaning against the wall of the porch. By comparison the two barns were sparkling white. I wondered if we should offer to stay in the barn during our one-nighter.

"David and Dorothy, it's so nice to meet you two," Lillie said, smiling and wiping her hands in her apron. "Fritz's sister has told me about you and how much she has been enjoying the summer and fall with you at the hotel."

Lillie was more cultured than expected for her part in the isolated western movie she was living. She had the calloused hands of the farming life, but she possessed genuine warmth that made you think you'd known her for years. She told us later that she and Fritz had met 20 years earlier when Fritz and his father sold beef to Lillie's family's restaurant over in Idaho Falls.

"Fritz, why don't you get a drink for David and I'll show Dorothy their room?" Lillie said, picking up one of Dorothy's bags and heading for the stairs.

"Beer OK?" Fritz asked, grabbing two from the fridge without bothering to wait for a reply. He popped the caps, handing one to me before heading into the living room where there was a yellow fire lapping up from an oversized fireplace.

"I hear you're an engineer," Fritz said, leaning back in his chair and looking into the flames. "We get lots of those up here for a week. Mostly we get citified greenhorns and five days later we send back men," Fritz said with a slight grin as he studied the bottle in his hand. "You wouldn't believe some of the stunts the city folks pull out here in the wild," he said, continuing to laugh as he told of a few anecdotal missteps by his guests. I didn't think it was worth interrupting since it sounded like Fritz was giving a speech he'd given many times. I decided it wasn't intended to degrade me or city folks, just to set the record straight as to where Fritz stood on the world outside the X Bar C Ranch.

"That engineering and drawing lines on paper wouldn't be any good for me," Fritz continued. "You know, with that kind of work you should sign up next year to come for one of our weeks at the ranch. We take folks through the work of a ranch, and they stay in the bunk house at the smaller of the two barns."

"I might give it a try," I said, "but I haven't been anyplace long enough to get vacation time. For now let's see how I do for just one day. How much is it for the five days?" I asked just to appear politely interested. After all, Dorothy and I were staying free for the night and eating their food as guests. There was no need getting on the wrong side of the rancher up here in the wilderness.

"Its $200 and you get three squares a day. My Lillie sees to that," Fritz said over his shoulder as he stepped back to the kitchen. "Ever ride a horse?" he asked from the other room.

"No, never had time," I said, "but I think I could learn if I had to."

He came through the door and handed me a second beer.

"There won't be any ridin' tomorrow but the week's stay involves plenty of ridin' through the wooded trails and every afternoon helping to round up the herd."

I was in pretty good shape so I wasn't concerned about the next day's adventure. I had been an all-state basketball player in high school and played intramurals in college. Besides, for crying out loud, I was 24-years-old. I wasn't sure how it related to the day but I'd also had the grit it took to survive growing up on Detroit's lower east side.

Lillie's tour ended at their guest room, which was clean and well decorated. Dorothy confirmed that it was their good luck that Lillie was in charge of the interior of the house and Fritz the outside. Dorothy and Lillie got along well from the start and they were going to stay at the house and visit the next day. Dorothy was particularly interested in seeing Lillie's collection of western scarves and hats she had made as well as a set of Indian woodcarvings. Fritz and I were going to travel to the upper 40 acres to bring down a load of hay. Based on what little of the mountains I had seen driving up to the ranch, I was looking forward to seeing the wonders of the Rockies in winter.

I awoke the next morning to the sounds of Lillie and Dorothy in the kitchen. Arriving downstairs at 6:00 am, I was informed that Fritz had already finished breakfast and was in the barn getting the horses and wagon ready for our adventure. I was allowed to wolf down two scrambled eggs and toast in about four minutes before being shooed out the door with a thermos of coffee and a soft muffin for the trail plus a sack lunch. A new layer of snow had fallen during the night and it crunched under my feet as I walked with some urgency toward the barn.

"Morning, David," Fritz said, more cheerily than was necessary as I approached the wagon. "I was worried the horses were going to take off without you."

"Good morning," I managed.

"Is that the warmest jacket you brought, son?" Fritz asked, as one asks a child of seven or eight if he remembered to bring his books to school.

"I'm fine," I claimed. "I've got three layers under this coat and I'm warm blooded." My coat was not as thick as I would have preferred but I wasn't about to give Fritz a victory for the day that hadn't even started. I'd be okay. It was a quiet snow-covered day of 20 degrees and the sun was shining. I squinted toward the sun and could see the tall pole-pines back of the house were giving only a hint of a breeze at their tips.

With a barely-disguised look of disgust, Fritz jumped down from the wagon and walked toward the house, returning a minute later with an extra coat for me. I climbed up on the wagon bench beside Fritz and held the coat in my lap.

"Ok, I guess everybody's ready," Fritz said, giving a flip to the reins and commanding, "Ted, Rusty, hay-yaa, let's go." The horses took a step and the wagon jerked forward, nearly throwing me off the bench.

We drove slowly at first through the crunching snow and down a ways to the edge of the snow-covered Wind River. The sound of the horses' hooves and the gentle clinking of the harnesses kept a soft steady rhythm. Chunks of soft snow shattered off the horses' backs as we turned right and traveled on a narrow road along the bank of the river. Ted and Rusty slowed into a steady pace as the road was mostly uphill. Once on the road Fritz seemed to mellow to the day. He turned quite pleasant, sometimes pausing to take in a sight when the road left the riverbank and climbed a ridge, and on another occasion stopping to point out the traces of a former Indian village.

"My dad knew many of the Indians around these woods and traded crops for pelts and trinkets with them. I still sell some of the stuff in our little gift shop. Dad moved here from Germany in 1906 with nothing but a dream of owning a ranch and living with his animals. He always said the animals were much easier to love and they never talked about you behind your back."

"How thick is the ice on the river?" I interrupted.

"Oh, it's plenty thick this time of year," Fritz said. "There's a point up here a ways where I cross to the meadow."

As we rode Fritz told me the story of how his dad had purchased the farm soon after emigrating. A year later he wrote to his brother about the beauty of the mountains and the peacefulness of the country. Fritz said his dad's brother read between the lines, sensing from the letter that his brother was lonely despite his love of America and the mountain life. Germany was not peaceful at the time and many were looking to escape to a safer place. His dad's brother wrote back mentioning his wife's younger sister Anne who his dad had known in school. Fritz's dad replied quickly to the unmarried sister. He said an exchange of letters for less than six months culminated in the sister moving to America and becoming his Dad's wife."

"I can see why you like living up here," I said, as the horses found a slower stride. "I'm afraid I'd get lonely for someone smarter than me to talk to, as well as a restaurant, a grocery, even a movie". I guessed Fritz had never lived anywhere else so these things probably weren't an issue for him.

"Seems like you found a lifestyle up here that's made for you," I said, just stirring the pot a bit, "but have you ever wondered what it would be like to live and work down below this mountain, say in Dubois, or Casper or maybe over in Cheyenne?" I was sure of his answer but I was wrong.

"Yea, I haven't always lived up here hiding on the mountain. I attended University of Iowa in Iowa City for three years majoring in Animal Husbandry," Fritz said to my surprise. "My grades were just so-so, partly because of working two jobs, but after my junior year it seemed I was on my way to Vet School for two more years. That would have been the river flowing through my life except I took an internship with a vet in Dubois and hated it. I found many people were too stupid to own a pet or a working animal. They brought animals to the clinic for things like 'sad eyes' or refusing to eat or running away from home. I'd run away too if they had been my owner."

"Sorry," I said. "I didn't mean you were hiding."

"Well, let's just say I found something up here smarter than I am to talk to every day – the animals," Fritz said.

Three deer broke out of the woods, leaping through the snowdrifts along the road and crossed just ahead of us. A few minutes later Fritz said he could hear a bear crashing through the snowy woods just up the hill from the road. Frankly I couldn't hear it over the sound of Ted and Rusty's breathing and the rattling harnesses.

In about a half hour we reached a gradual slope toward the river and Fritz announced it was the crossing point. He eased the horses and the wagon down the bank and onto the frozen river. I could feel the horses adjust to shorter steps on the snow-covered ice as they started pulling us across. We traveled about a hundred feet across the Wind River where we pulled up the bank and into Fritz's hay meadow. Stacked in small pyramids under the snow, the field of rectangular hay bales reminded me of rows of three-layer cakes covered in white icing. I didn't mention the visual to my host.

Fritz drove to the nearest pyramid and we started disassembling the cakes and loading the bales on the wagon. We loaded from the ground until we had a solid platform on the wagon. Then Fritz stood on the ground and heaved the bales to me standing in the wagon. We alternated positions until we couldn't throw the bales high enough to reach the top of the load. Fritz was surprised that I knew how to load a hay wagon full. I'd spent three summers haying near my family's cabin in northern Michigan. Nonetheless, it was heavy work as the bales were frozen and I wasn't used to such all-out exercise. Conversation was limited at 9,300 feet to conserve our energy and we were soon down to our shirtsleeves. When we finished loading the wagon, Fritz removed the bits from the bridles so the horses could feed through the snow. We brushed off a cake of hay and took a break for sandwiches and hot coffee.

The enormity of the snow-covered pines and mountains as far as you could see, with the Grand Tetons in the distance, gave me a better understanding of why a person living here would find a way to stay. The sky was deep blue and the snow was so clean you could eat it to quench your thirst. The migratory birds had flown south but the jays wolfed down our bread crusts. We gradually added layers of clothing as we cooled off. I think Fritz and I were equally glad for the lunch break.

After lunch we re-hitched the horses' bridles and started the return trip. Ted and Rusty, feeling the new weight, struggled to get started but moved steadily once the wheels broke loose from their position.

"The other thing that kept me from being a vet," Fritz said, as if there had been only a few seconds between conversations rather than two hours, "was that Dad got sick and I had to run the ranch. Mother had died the year before I started school, and when Dad died Lillie and I were left to manage the ranch." He looked up and turned his head slowly from side to side taking in the scene. "Can't say as I miss the city too much."

So there it was, I thought, as the horses struggled to high-step through the drifted snow. Fritz claimed to be a man with a plan and a place where he was meant to be. It sounded a little too smooth to me but quite appealing. I had recently graduated from college and had been working in construction trying to decide if I wanted to enlist in the military or be drafted the following year. Based on news reports that fall and winter, it seemed the U.S. would soon be forced to join the war in Europe and possibly elsewhere. A year down the road I could be dropping bombs over Germany, patrolling the Pacific, or resting in my place below the earth. The ranch was an interesting place to visit and I didn't envy Fritz's life, only the fact that he had found it. I certainly hadn't found my place in life or even the road leading toward it.

"Fritz, you've got a good thing going here," I said, with surprising candor. We had descended the slippery bank and were proceeding across the river. As we neared the middle of the river I said, "It's interesting to see a life so different from the one Dorothy and I have started. We are still trying to find out what we want to be when we grow up. Sometimes I think..."

Suddenly, there was a loud crack from below the snow. The ice shattered and the wagon started tilting forward. I watched in what seemed like slow motion as the two horses and the front wheels of the wagon plunged down through the ice into the river. I could see slow spikes of freezing spray erupting high into the air. The horses let out a shrill cry, holding their heads high and thrashing about wildly in the hole in the ice.

Fritz and I were only saved from going in by grabbing the seat rails. I was too stunned to move but Fritz jumped up and stood on the back of the bench, immediately taking off his boots and pants, ripping off his clothes down to his skivvies. He yelled for me to do the same. The sun was close to hiding behind the mountains and I was shivering even with my clothes on so I wondered what the hell he was thinking.

"Are you nuts?" I asked.

"Get out of those clothes," Fritz shouted louder. Then he jumped feet first into the river between the horses, holding their heads together, talking to them and trying to keep them calm. He looked back and shouted for me to kick the bales off the wagon and spread them around the hole. The wagon was creating a bigger hole as it moved up and down in the current. Sheer terror injected me with limitless energy as I tore off my clothes, kicked some of the bales to the ice and jumped off the rear of the wagon. He yelled for me to throw our clothes on the upriver bales along with my socks which were the only things, other than my skivvies, I hadn't removed. I ran around spreading the bales on the ice not allowing myself to think about how cold I was.

Fritz went under water to free the horses from the wagon. It took a couple of plunges to get each horse free. Fritz was blue as he broke through the surface the final time, sputtering and choking, flailing his arms up at me.

"Throw me a rope. It's under the seat," Fritz shouted, shaking the icy water from his hair and struggling to hold the horses' reins.

He tied Rusty, the upriver horse, to the wagon so he wouldn't get pushed by the current and crash into Ted. This caused Ted to float a foot or so higher in the water. I stretched out my arm to Fritz and helped him climb up out of the hole.

"We need to time the surges of the river," he said. Ted floated sideways to the hole and I was able to grab his tail. Just then, Ted floated up to the point that Fritz could pull and twist the horse's head over on the ice. I stood as far from the break as I could get and pulled on Ted's tail. The horse was thrashing in the water and his eyes were wide as he fell back into the river.

At that moment I thought Fritz was going to get the four of us killed. All I could think of was how the news reports were going to describe the scene the next day. "Officials were mystified today when they found two naked men and their horses frozen to death up on Wind River."

Fritz kept talking to Ted and telling him he could make it up on the ice. He reached up and rubbed the horse's forehead. Ted's black eyes were full of fear and as big as 8-balls. Then the horse floated a bit higher and Ted lunged, hooking his front hooves up on top of the ice.

"Come on Ted. That's it. You can do it," Fritz said, patting the side of the horse's face. "Come on Teddy, get a back leg up!" he yelled, pulling the horse's head. On the next surge Ted clawed and slid up on the ice. Fritz kept talking to his horse and lay on top of him for a moment.

There was no time to rest or try to dry off as Rusty was struggling against the force of the river and the ropes. Fritz jumped back in the water and untied Rusty from the wagon. He bounced him in the water as he floated upward. Fritz got out of the water and pulled Rusty's head and neck as the river surged. Fritz told me later that Rusty was more skittish of the two so he had rescued Ted first to show Rusty it could be done.

We made many more tries but Rusty didn't seem to have the strength to climb out of the hole and the struggle was making him weaker. I thought we might have to leave the horse to save ourselves. Then Fritz started yelling at Rusty and me and Rusty somehow climbed up and was lying up on the ice. We were so exhausted that we were barely able to slide Rusty away from the hole.

"Can we get dressed yet," I asked, although I didn't know if it would help. Without answering Fritz jumped in the water again and dived to release the wagon tongue. It turns out, fortunately, that western wagons are made to hitch the tongue at either end.

"Damn!" Fritz said as he emerged from the water with the tongue. "It's cold under there." Looking toward me he said, "There are natural springs that crop up under the river from time to time and weaken the ice. It never happened before but I guess we found one."

We were both in the process of freezing to death and I didn't give a damn why we had almost plunged to our imminent, frozen death. We struggled to put our dry clothes on and Fritz lit a fire with matches he had in his shirt pocket.

"Up here, in the mountains my friend," he said, as we stood close enough to the bale that was ablaze to set our clothes on fire, "we learn to save the horses so they can save us, and above all else we learn to keep our clothes dry."

Ted and Rusty somehow got to their feet once the fire got going. Fritz asked me to walk them until they looked dry. I walked the two work horses back to the meadow and rubbed them with dry hay. At Fritz's signal I had to coax them back down the slope and onto the ice.

Fritz had untangled the harnesses and attached the wagon tongue to the back of the wagon and unloaded the rest of the hay. Fritz found a downed pole-pine to use as a lever to lift what was now the rear of the wagon. I sat on one end of the pole and placed it over a bale of hay with the other end in the water under the back of the wagon. Fritz yelled for me to take my clothes off again as I was going to be getting soaked when the wagon moved up and down at the end of the pole. I did as I was told. At this point he was dressed and I wasn't. I shuttered to think of what the 11 o'clock news would say about this scene.

Fritz put the harnesses on the horses and hitched them to the tongue of the wagon. He stood in front of the horses and talked quietly to them. He signaled me to sit on the lever pole. Then he gradually raised his voice encouraging the team to pull the wagon out of the river. The horses pulled and gashed at the ice, slipping to their knees then standing and pulling again. A water spout erupted from the hole dousing me into a pink popsicle.

Holding the reins, Fritz reached down to rub the horses' bloody knees and we rested a minute. Frozen as solid as the ice I was standing on, I got back on the pole and tried to bounce for better leverage. At the same time Fritz shouted words of encouragement to the horses. The wagon jumped up on the edge of the break and crashed through the ice, making a bigger hole and throwing me into the water. Despite thinking that I was already frozen blue, the river was a shock and I had no breath as I thrashed about under the wagon. I banged my head on something hard, probably a wheel, and dove to find the hole in the ice. In my panic I dove toward the front of the wagon instead of toward the hole. Dying and sinking slowly toward my end I saw Dorothy's face. My feet touched the rocky river bottom and I pushed off coming up banging my head on the ice and desperately trying to find a pocket of air. I hoped Dorothy would understand that I tried with every ounce of my strength to get back to her. I could hear the horses stomping and tearing at the ice above me and I turned toward the back end of the wagon. Bursting through the surface, choking and deep into oxygen debt, I was scared, frozen and, I must admit, mad as hell. Fritz grabbed my arm and pulled me over the edge of the break onto the ice. I lay there still thinking I would die, but now at least it would be easier to find the body.

Suddenly there was a huge explosion of water and ice and the wagon jumped over the edge of the hole and rested on the surface. The horses had continued jumping and pulling even after Fritz had gone to save me.

Revived a little by the horses' successful struggle, I fumbled to put on my dry clothes. Buttons were impossible with frozen hands. I couldn't feel life in any of my body parts. Fritz put a half load of the dry hay back on the wagon and we walked the horses to the shore. As the sun's warmth left us on our own, we climbed up to the bench and Fritz signaled the horses to take us home. On our way down the mountain Fritz and I suddenly became too tired and too cold to sit up on the bench and hold the reins. Fritz dug a hole in the hay and crawled in where he seemed to collapse. I couldn't feel my feet so I put them down in the hole, accidentally hitting Fritz on the head with the heels of my boots. He took my boots off then opened his coat and hugged my feet as he either fell asleep or passed out.

The pace of the horses was easy on the road, which was mostly downhill. I saw three young men walking in front of us on the road but when I called to them they disappeared. I was aware of the sound of birds' wings in flight but couldn't see any birds. These images stayed with me all the way down the mountain and they live with me even today.

Delirious, I dropped the reins and the horses plodded along while Fritz and I were in our hypothermia-induced sleep. Next thing I knew, Lillie and Dorothy were running to meet the wagon and pulling us down, helping us into the house. Fritz protested, insisting he needed to tend to the horses, but Lillie put his arm over her shoulder and marched him into the house, dropping him in a chair in front of the fire. Dorothy helped me inside to a seat close to the fireplace. The hot fire stung my feet and hands and I couldn't stop the tears. Meanwhile, the ladies unbridled the lifesaving horses, put them in their stables and fed them before tending further to their men.

Shaking, as I sat in front of the crackling fire, I looked over at my host whose eyes were closed. When he looked at me a moment later, his eyes were as glazed as mine. Fritz had been right. Ted and Rusty had taken us home. Fritz was also right about keeping our clothes dry. I wasn't convinced we could have been any more frozen coming down the mountain on that December afternoon, but I knew that wet clothing would have resulted in the horses delivering two corpses encased in ice to our widows. My host's advice and knowledge of the elements had saved our lives.

The ice in my hair was melting, forming puddles near my feet as I hung my head, elbows leaning heavily on my knees. It would be hours before I regained any normal feeling in my feet, but they were starting to really hurt and Fritz said that was a good sign. I had certainly learned a great deal in one day at the ranch. I was not sure I could survive a week up on the mountain but I knew I'd learn a lot about ranching, and myself, if I did.

Sixty-eight years later my fingers still freeze at temperatures as high as 50 degrees, and sometimes I hear birds in the sky and there are none when I look for them. I still remember very clearly those frightening moments that day on the road, on the ice, and under it. I'm thankful to God and to Fritz, Ted and Rusty for getting me through the day alive.

Author's Note: This story is based on conversations with David Wood at 92 years of age. Nearly 70 years earlier David spent a harrowing day at the X Bar C Ranch along the Wind River in Wyoming.

Family Fire

By Steven R. Roberts

A light snow had been falling all afternoon and Jim was glad to be back in his New Yorker. The seven-year-old car had been in for repairs and Jim had a fellow worker drop him off at the dealership. As he drove home, lighter, smaller vehicles were sliding all over the road. Jim stroked his trim salt and pepper beard and checked it as he adjusted the rear view mirror. The beard was a new addition; one Jim thought would take the emphasis off his rapidly retreating hair line.

Jim had been looking forward to surviving the week and spending some time working on a woodturning project he had been trying to find time to complete. He was halfway through making a floor-length table lamp out of a piece of birch that used to be the shade tree at the west corner of their front yard. The chance for a little creativity and the low droning sound of the lathe would allow him to relax and forget the pressure of his work week. But all of that went out the window when Jim's wife called earlier that afternoon.

Anna had called with two items but Jim had talked her out of a grocery stop due to the weather. She agreed they could get by with what they had in the house. Anna had also relayed the message from Jim's mother's earlier phone call.

"She mentioned that your father has not been feeling well all week," Anna said. "Your mom asked if we could come up and help with some of the chores at the farm."

"What about their friend at the next farm to the east?" Jim asked, trying to hold the frustration in his voice.

"Well, I guess he must be out of town. I don't know. I didn't want to ask. Besides, your mother sounded depressed at the situation," Anna said. "I told her we'd be happy to get out of the city and come for a visit. What else could I say?"

God bless my wife, Jim thought. Her heart was in the right place but he really didn't want to start out for the farm first thing on Saturday. Maybe it would snow so much during the night that they couldn't plow themselves out of the driveway in the morning. In any event, the weather was getting worse and Jim was glad to turn down Elmwood and pull safely into his driveway.

The home was a comfortable ranch with white siding that Jim had extended by adding a second garage four years earlier. He had also converted a room in the basement into a bedroom for their son, Eddie. The room provided the 14-year-old with space for his junk and the privacy the teen craved and vice versa for his parents and two younger children living upstairs.

It was good to see Eddie had been out with the snow blower. The driveway and sidewalks were clear except for the light snow still falling. Eddie had been a dream to raise until he turned 13. Then he had switched into the normal, sometimes distracted and moody teenager more interested in the wisdom of his learned peers than the advice and guidance from his parents. He was still lovable but less focused on his studies and the other longer term goals his parents had in mind.

Jim waved to a neighbor shoveling his driveway as he hit the button to open the garage door. The trip home in the snow had allowed Jim time to accept his obligation to visit his parents the next day. The blowing snow had also prevented Jim from noticing smoke coming from the New Yorker's engine compartment. Once in the garage, however, Jim noticed what he thought was steam coming from under the hood. How the engine could overheat in this weather was a wonder to Jim as he came to a stop in the garage.

Eddie usually hung the small snow blower on two nails at the end of the garage so it was about three feet up on the wall. Because the snow was still falling Eddie had just leaned the machine against the wall. Jim inadvertently tapped the snow blower with his bumper as he pulled to a stop and opened his door. He waved to Anna, standing in the doorway to the house.

"Hi, hon," Anna said through the screen door from the kitchen. "Jim, look. I think there's still something wrong with the car," Anna said as she noticed smoke coming through the car grill.

"Hi, honey," Jim said, ducking back into the car for his suit coat and briefcase.

"Jim, the car's on fire!" Anna shouted, seeing yellow flames suddenly lapping through the grill. At that instant the flames ignited the dripping gasoline from the punctured plastic fuel tank on the snow blower. The car's bumper had crushed the edge of a bracket into the wall rupturing the gas tank.

"Anna!" Jim shouted, as he took a step toward the front of the car. The explosion blasted a hole in the garage wall and blew Jim into the air, causing him to throw his suit coat and briefcase in the air. He landed into the two trashcans. With his clothes and hair on fire, Jim was blinded by the flames and he put one arm up over his face. Struggling to stand, he fell back to the floor screaming in pain.

"Anna, get back in the house," Jim shouted, writhing on the floor, beating the flames with his hands. Reaching for his face, he realized his beard and eyebrows had been set on fire by his flaming shirt and tie.

The explosion had covered Anna with flames, blowing her back into the house. In shock and on fire, she fell down the basement stairs, breaking her left arm and her right wrist. Her dress and hair were on fire as she reached the bottom of the stairs, screaming her son's name. Eddie untangled himself from the bed, where he had been reading, and ran toward his mother.

"Mom, what's happening?" Eddie yelled as he reached the bottom of the steps.

"Get dad, for God's sake, get dad, he's on fire!" Anna screamed.

"Mom, you're on fire," Eddie said, burning his hands as he slapped at the fire in his mother's hair. He ran for a pillow from his bed and returned, pounding his mother over and over to smother the flames. Anna cried out with every blow. Her eyes would not open as she sat waving her arms toward the stairs and cried out, "Eddie, get dad. He's on fire," she repeated.

"Mom, where is he?" Eddie shouted as he stepped over his mother and started up the stairs toward the rolling black smoke pouring down from the first floor.

"Dad's hurt and laying in the garage," Anna cried. "Oh, my God, the kids, get the kids out." She collapsed against the wall and put a hand over her burned eyelids and slapped at her hair with the other hand until she could smell the flesh of her hand burning.

"Dad, Dad!" Eddie screamed as loud as he could, feeling the intense heat as he reached the first floor.

He held onto the kitchen door and took a step into the garage shouting for his father. Through the black smoke he saw Jim across the hood of the car, trying to beat out the flames in his clothes. Eddie's dad was struggling to stand by holding on to the garbage cans, which were in the process of collapsing from the heat.

"Dad!" Eddie shouted, taking a step into the garage. Through the smoke he could make out a look of fear and desperation in his father's eyes.

Eddie started to call out again just as the two spare gas cans exploded one after the other, filling the garage with flames engulfing his dad and the New Yorker. Eddie's face and t-shirt were on fire and he was blown back through the screen door into the house, falling down the stairs and landing finally on his unconscious mother. Eddie jumped over his mother and ran to his bedroom. He slid over the bed, cranking open the escape window his father had installed. He returned to pick up his mother's limp body and stuffed her out the window. He crawled out and put his hands under her arms in a bear hug and dragged her up out of the window well and across the back yard, away from the house. Her smoldering hair was in his face and the smell, or maybe it was the whirling calamity about him, suddenly made Eddie feel sick. He turned his head and threw up in the snow. Taking a few more steps, Eddie lowered his mother into a sitting position on the bottom of the sliding board. He lowered her slowly to the curve of the sliding board.

"I'll be back, Mom," Eddie said, starting around the house to the front yard, his bleeding bare feet leaving prints in the snow. As he crossed the driveway, the two garages were being consumed in flames and thick smoke was filling the house and yard.

"Dad, Daddy!" he yelled toward the garages. He ran to the garage and pounded on the door nearest the house. It was red hot and burned his clenched fists. He moved to the door on the added garage and grabbed the garage door handle, trying desperately to pull it up. The handle burned his hand and he yelled again for his father. He paused to listen but heard only the crackling roar of the fire from within.

"Daaaad!" Eddie screamed in agony, but there was no reply. Standing with his hands pushing against the door, Eddie became dizzy from the rain of horror falling down around him. Was everything and everyone going to be lost? He was driven by a desperate need to save someone, something.

He ran to the front door trying to reach his little brother and sister but the smoke drove him back outside. Eddie's lungs were burning as he jumped the piles of snow along the driveway and ran across the front yard.

Inside the garage, Jim had been trying to pull himself off the floor when he heard Eddie calling his name from the kitchen doorway. He raised his arm to warn his son, just as the two gas cans exploded. The blast pushed Jim sideways through the door into the second garage where he slumped against the front bumper of the family's van. That's where he was a few moments later when he heard Eddie calling his name again, this time from out front.

With the original garage totally in flames, Jim knew he had to get out before the gas tank in the New Yorker exploded, flattening the west end of the house. Jim could hear his son beating on the garage door as he struggled to get to his feet. He got to his knees and reached up grabbing the half-finished lamp being held in the chuck. Spitting and choking in black smoke, Jim opened his mouth to call out to his son to stay clear of the garage but he managed only a halting dry whisper. He felt his way along the side of the vehicle, stumbling toward the front of the garage. His eyes were burning from the heat as he lunged with his hand, punching the garage door opener switch, which had been rendered useless by the fire.

Outside, Eddie rounded the corner of the east end of the house. He could see Penny, his red headed six-year-old sister, pounding on her bedroom window and yelling for help. Penny's room was filling up with smoke and Eddie could see the pleading terror in her tear-filled blue eyes. She had been playing "dress up" with her mother's clothes at the time of the first explosion and was wearing one of Anna's old pink ruffled dresses as well as an old necklace, earrings and red lipstick. Eddie ran up to the house and pounded on the window.

"Penny, I'll get you out," Eddie yelled, not sure if his sister could hear him through two panes of glass and the roar of the fire. "Where's Bobby? Is he with you? Penny, hang on! Can you get a chair and unlock the window?" Penny just sobbed as she banged her fists against the window and stared wide eyed pleading with Eddie.

Eddie picked up two small branches poking up through the snow and threw them at the window. He grabbed a handful of dirt from under the bushes and threw it. The Plexiglas storm window wouldn't break and the sound scared Penny back into the room. When she returned, Eddie could see Bobby, the three-year-old, jumping and screaming beside her. Bobby's terrified face and big eyes were all that was visible above the windowsill except for his outstretched arms. They were both being blanketed with black smoke as they yelled and pounded on the window, pleading for help.

"Edo, Edo, Edooo, help!" Eddie could read their lips as they cried the favorite name for their big brother. "Help us, Edo," Penny said, tears running a thin trail through the soot on her cheeks.

Eddie ran toward the back yard, past his mother lying motionless on the sliding board. A light layer of snow was causing steam to rise from her body. The snow was also starting to cover the two black tracks leading from the basement window. Eddie grabbed two large logs from the family's stack of firewood. He ran back to the window and motioned for his brother and sister to back away from the window. He attempted to throw the logs at the window as hard as he could. One log hit the side of the house and one fell short. The logs proved to be too heavy for Eddie to throw with any force toward the window. With no time to go back for smaller logs, Eddie threw them again and they both bounced to the snow. He threw them again and again. Sometimes he hit the window and sometimes his aim was off. The logs landed at his feet and Eddie went to his knees to pick up the logs and threw them from there. Just then the garage at the other end of the house exploded, causing Penny and Bobby to look back into the house and hug each other. They screamed and started jumping in fright as a burst of black smoke and debris flew into the room, some pieces striking the window.

Eddie's brother and sister turned back with their hands pressed against the window as if trying to push it out. Bobby was looking up to Penny pleading for help and alternating between pushing at the glass and wrapping his arms around his sister's waist and burying his face in her gown. Eddie threw the logs again and they didn't flinch. He bent down to pick up the logs and this time he looked up to see the kids' hands slide down the window. First Bobby's hands disappeared and then Penny's. There was a streak of red lipstick down the glass where Penny had been pressing her face hard against the window.

The whole house was in flames as Eddie held the logs up toward the sky, crying. "Why, why?" he said sobbing. He heard the sirens stop as the first fire truck pulled up in front of the house. Eddie was sitting on his knees, hugging the two logs, slumped over with his head in the snow on the ground. His eyes were closed and tears were freezing on his red cheeks as a firefighter approached.

"Son, are you alright?" the fireman asked.

"Yes," Eddie whispered.

"Is there anyone in the house?"

"In there," Eddie sobbed, pointing toward the window. "And sir," Eddie said, leaning back on his heels and looking up into the snow, which was heavier now, "my Mom's in the back yard under the snow on the swing set. I'm not sure if she's alive. Please hurry."

Eddie's father was found slumped against the garage door and Penny and little Bobby were found holding each other at the base of the window in Penny's bedroom. Anna and Eddie were taken to the hospital where they were admitted for smoke inhalation and third-degree burns. They recovered well enough physically to be released in four and six days respectively. Mother and son moved in temporarily with Jim's parents on the farm.

Author's note: Unfortunately, this is a true story. The names have been changed and dialog has been added around the events in the local fire marshal's report on the fire. A special thanks also goes to Rollin Kerzee, retired Lima, Ohio, fire investigator for comments on this story.

Rescued

By Chrissie Bowman

In late October, 2000, I could hear the leaves crunch underneath my feet as I walked across my front lawn. It was early afternoon, the fall air was crisp. Leaves were burning somewhere in the distance. Fall is my favorite time of year. Dogs were barking. I could hear the dogs from the horse farm across the road. They were coming to greet me. The horses chattering to each other with their whinnies was comforting. It was so peaceful, just far enough away from the city to be country, but still close enough to town for last-minute shopping.

The dogs, Prince and Charity, black and red Dobermans, were rescued from a puppy mill by their owner. They were scrawny, undernourished and very timid the first time I met them. You could tell they had a rough beginning in life but they had fattened up in the two years since I met them. Prince looked very intimidating with his pointy ears and thick studded collar, a sharp contrast to his real personality. Charity, on the other hand, was a very delicate red Dobe, with a graceful presence about her. They both seemed to know they were rescued and tried very hard to please their owners.

For some strange reason these two dogs had grown attached to my three children. Prince and Charity would make their daily visit across the road to give kisses to the kids, or gently take little scraps of whatever the kids could find out of their chubby, dimpled hands.

This was a week that the kids spent with their father and the days and nights were rough without them. I tried to explain to the dogs that the kids weren't home. They looked at me as if they understood, but still they searched the yard for the chubby little kids that loved them.

I ran in the mornings just to get the day started. It was four and a half miles down to the Fenway farm and back, my time, my alone time to sort things out. My divorce, although two years old, still stung like it was a fresh knife wound.

The road we lived on was busier than normal that summer. The diesel smell was overwhelming. The main road had been closed for two months for construction and the semi trucks that had been diverted down our road interrupted the fall air with a pungent diesel smell. Their loud horns blaring as Prince and Charity narrowly escaped yet another massive front bumper. I held my breath each time. It scared me to think how I would ever explain to my kids if something happened to those two dogs. I locked the dogs in my fenced-in backyard as I had done several times before in the last couple of months, hoping to keep them from harm's way while their owners were at work and while I went for my run.

As I ran I thought of my kids. I could not stand to be away from them. Is anyone throwing the ball to Dakota? How about reading Georgia's favorite story to her? Does Savannah have her blankie? A thousand thoughts overwhelmed me. They are my world. They would return to me the next day. I repeated the thought of them returning over and over in my mind. When I looked up, I was back home. Four and a half miles went pretty fast, but now the clock seemed to tick slower.

I checked on the dogs; they were asleep in the sun in the backyard, safe. I went inside to wind down. Nothing was on TV but sob stories of child abuse and neglect on the talk shows. I couldn't concentrate. The house was so empty. I would have given anything to hear the kids fight, cry, anything was better than silence.

I hate my divorce, I hate that my kids had to leave for days at a time, I hate my ex-husband, I hate everything. I decided to get busy doing something; I couldn't stay inside, just looking at all the toys. It made me cry. I went outside. The lawn didn't need mowing, the leaves had been raked. I went across the road to visit the horses. They were such peaceful animals. My neighbors had let me help feed them on occasion. It was a huge production, feeding and watering over one hundred horses. It took a small crew to finish the job every evening. All the horses had been rescued from another country where they were to be auctioned off for human consumption. Gross, the thought had sickened me. I went back home, decided to clean out my gutters. I used my truck to jump up on my garage roof then I had to climb higher with my broom in hand to reach the top of the roof. Once on top, I sat amazed by the beauty in the leaves already turning their fall colors.

Prince and Charity had spotted me. I'm sure they wondered what in the world I was doing, as I threw handfuls of leaves from the gutters to the ground. I was almost finished. Only 10 or 15 feet to go around the backside of the house and I would have been done. The dogs sat peacefully watching me. I could still hear the trucks whizzing by the house. I talked to the dogs, my only companions. I told them I would let them out soon but they didn't seem concerned and went back to basking in the last of the fall sun.

I had started to climb again, to reach my broom that I had tossed to the peak of the roof, but I quickly lost my footing on the slippery roof. I flattened out on the roof shingles, trying to find something to stop my slide. I heard screaming, loud, long, painful screaming. Soon I realized it was my own voice. I fell off of the roof onto a solid piece of cold earth. It felt like slow motion, the screaming, the crying, falling through the air then nothing but silence. I lay on the hard ground. No one heard my cries for help, no one came. It was the country and no one was around, no one but the dogs.

Prince and Charity must have sensed I was in trouble because once I had calmed down and just lay there they both came to me, smelling me, licking my face with their warm kisses. I couldn't move. For some reason I could not get my body to move. I tried to get up but my legs wouldn't listen to me. I was overwhelmed with exhaustion and just wanted to sleep. Tired and cold, I was still in my sweatshirt, shorts and running shoes.

I woke up from time to time to the loud moaning, howling of Charity. She was at the back corner of the fenced backyard. She wouldn't stop howling. It bothered me. I yelled at her, "Shut up Charity!" I just wanted silence, so I could sleep. As much as I begged her to stop she just kept howling and moaning. Prince was right beside me; almost lying on top of me. Every now and then he would shower me with wet kisses, nudging my face with his. It was really annoying. They didn't understand that I just wanted to be left alone. Why had I even bothered to lock them in the fence? I just wanted to sleep. That is what I needed.

Hours had passed. It was getting colder. Each time I'd wake up, it would be darker and colder. I was awake now, wide-awake. I wanted to go inside to get warm and to stop shivering. Prince was trying to keep me warm, and Charity was calling for help. I realized that at that moment. I wanted to get up, go inside and call for help, but if I could do that I wouldn't need help. My thoughts were distorted. I shivered.

I thought of my kids. I began to cry. Have I been a good parent? I could do better. I hadn't always put them first in the last couple of years. Why? I was selfish. I should just close my eyes and go to sleep forever. I was so concerned about my thoughts and feelings. I had wanted to date someone, anyone. I wanted to have someone make me feel good about myself. I'd leave the kids with sitters. I'd pick up extra work. I hated their dad for doing this to me.

I couldn't feel my legs. I realized at that moment that all the sleeping I had been doing was my body going into shock from the trauma of the fall and the cold. I'm a nurse, I knew better than to sleep. I started talking out loud to the dogs. They listened. Charity came to me every once in a while, checking me out. Prince was still at my side, he never left me. It was getting dark. My thoughts rambled through my head.

"How long have I been out here?" I asked the dogs. It felt like forever. I heard a noise, a familiar noise. It was those stupid trucks. No, it was the tractors across the road. They must be feeding the horses. It was suppertime. I knew the schedule for feeding the horses.

I started yelling for help. Louder and louder, I wanted help. I'm going to get help, for me and my kids. I would not let my ex-husband win. I would not let hatred win. I prayed. I prayed to God harder than I've ever prayed.

"Please, God, save me," I pleaded. "I'll change, I promise. I'll be a better Mom, I'll be a better person, I promise, God, please save me, kids first, I promise." Over and over I pleaded. I would never use the word hate again. No more bad thoughts, I promise.

I tried to move but something was under my lower back, something hard, like a rock. When I reached down I felt my shoe, and it was still attached to my foot, but I couldn't feel my legs. I tried to pull myself with my elbows. I couldn't feel my legs. I think I was lying in my own urine. Why couldn't I feel anything? My arms were okay. I told Prince we needed Jack, the dog's owner, to come help. Prince seems to understand, he was standing over me. I realized how warm he was keeping me. I could still hear the tractors. I only had one hour. It took about an hour to feed and water the horses. I began to pray again.

"God, save me, please," I begged.

Prince wanted me to pet him. He kept nudging my hand. He wanted something. I knew at that moment he was going to help me. I grabbed his heavy collar with both hands and he began dragging me slowly, gently. He could sense I was hurt. Charity was barking, louder than I had ever heard her bark. She ran all over the yard, excited, she wanted someone to see her, to see us. Prince pulled me a few inches at a time. His strong Doberman body strained to pull me. We inched a path across the back yard and turned at the corner of the house. After what seemed like forever we were at the gate. He had pulled me at least 40 feet. I talked to Prince like I would one of my kids. I pointed up at the gate latch indicating how he could nudge open the gate with his nose. Prince and Charity both were prancing impatiently at the gate. I begged them to find Jack. I needed help. After several tries, Prince popped open the fence gate latch. He and Charity started to run out, but they had both stopped to lick my face. Then they were gone. I watched them dart toward the road as they always did, but this time it seemed as if they stopped to look before they crossed the road.

Just a few minutes passed and Jack was standing above me, calling 911. Prince and Charity were back, licking my face. They had rescued me. They returned their favor. They had been rescued dogs and now they rescued me.

It has been 10 years since my accident. My prognosis was poor when I reached the hospital - never to walk or have feeling restored completely in my legs, or even work as a nurse again. It took me a long time to learn to walk right again. I was rescued in more ways than one that October day 2000.

After surgery and many long months and hours of physical therapy I was back to normal, for the most part. I have learned a lot from my accident. My life has changed completely. Hate is no longer in my vocabulary. My kids come first, always. I have continued my nursing career, helping to care for post-operative orthopedic patients. I have since moved from that house in the country but I've been back to see Prince and Charity a few times. We have a bond. We've all three been rescued.

Guest Author Bio: Chrissie Bowman is a single mom raising three teenagers; the oldest graduated from high school this year and will be attending the University of Kentucky. Chrissie has been working as an LPN for the past 15 years and is currently back in school furthering her education.

Rita's Ride to Remember

By Steven R. Roberts

I stared at the freezing rain hitting the thin windows of the bus door and watched the highway traffic splash by. I was sitting on the steps of a crowded northbound bus up next to the driver. It wasn't the usual place to have a meaningful life experience, I suppose, but this ride made a difference in who I was and who I am today, nearly 40 years later.

It was December, 1963, and I had just finished finals for my first quarter at a Carolina university. It had been an important four months, full of learning experiences in and out of the classroom. Campuses across the country were involved in civil rights demonstrations and the beginning of the Vietnam War protest movement that would take on its own life later in the decade.

It hadn't been surprising that I stayed in my dorm room during the civil rights protests that fall. I don't know where my level-of-rage gauge was set at that time, but I chose not to get involved in the civil rights events on campus, at least not in a marching way. Growing up in Connecticut, I hadn't been sensitized to the plight of blacks, particularly those living in the south. In addition to that, my parents hadn't sacrificed to send me to college so I could get arrested.

In my safe world up north, I thought the minority issues in the south would work themselves out. As long as I wasn't discriminating, I wasn't part of the problem and didn't need to be part of the solution. But down south, around halfway through my first quarter, there was a student-led civil rights protest that started on the green in front of my dorm. It really wasn't a violent gathering down below my fourth floor window, more noise and signs than action, but both of my roommates along with another friend got arrested and carted off to jail that evening.

The next day I talked to two of my professors about the situation with the arrests of my friends. Knowing the girls would be in danger of flunking out if they didn't study for the mid-term tests; both professors agreed the girls should be given a chance to study the pre-test materials. They also agreed that I could deliver the study materials to the girls at the jail. To that day, I had never known anybody who had been in jail, so it was understandable that I had to steel my nerves to enter the city's main police station.

"I've come to visit my friends," I explained to the officer at the front desk. "They are missing their study time for mid-term exams and I am here to give them some test materials."

"You want them to study in jail?" the officer, a large black man, asked. "Do you have any idea what it is like in jail, miss?"

"No, of course not, but I know they are pretty tough girls and I'm sure they can find a table or a corner to sit in while they study. I've brought three pencils. They'll want to take notes," I said, handing the pencils over the counter.

The officer stood slowly and smiled, looking into my eyes. I blinked several times involuntarily.

"You mistake tough for stupid, young lady," he spit out the words. "Now, why don't you and your honky friends just stay out of the business of those of us who live down here in the south? We black folks can take care of ourselves just fine without you-all comin' down here and sticking your lily white noses in where they don't belong."

He reached across the counter and swept up the three envelopes containing the tests and laid them on his desk next to the pencils. He sat back down at his desk and never looked my way again.

I found out later the girls weren't told I had come to see them and they never saw the study materials. The desk officer's outburst had caught me by surprise and it stung. I had thought the protest event and my three friends had been trying to help the officer's people. Clearly, the civil rights movement was more complicated than I had realized. Walking back to campus, I made a mental note to look up the word "honky."

There were many learning experiences that first few months of college. Among other things, I definitely became more aware and more sensitive to the civil rights movement that was engulfing the country's main streets and campuses. Earlier that year, George Wallace had been elected governor of Alabama on the slogan, "Segregation now, segregation tomorrow, segregation forever." That year President Kennedy promised a civil rights bill and Martin Luther King Jr. gave his, "I have a dream," speech. One of my roommates had managed to travel to Washington, D C to hear Reverend King speak.

Trying to make sure I survived my first semester at school, these events meant more to me now that I was living in the south. Things were changing at a fast pace and about to change even more. When President Kennedy was assassinated two days before Thanksgiving, the campus and the country shut down. Was it the president's stand on civil rights? Or was it the communists? Was it Vietnam? Or was it just a nut case.

Regardless, I wanted to get home as soon as possible the day I finished my finals in December. At 6:15 that evening, exhausted from staying up too late studying for my Finals, I bought a ticket at the Greyhound station and waited for the bus to arrive. The station was filled mostly with black people. I thought they might be going to Washington to visit the president's gravesite. When the bus to Hartford was called I gathered my books and bags and headed outside looking for bus number 1314.

I spotted it and got in line to board. The bus had been half full when it arrived and the remaining seats were being claimed by those ahead of me. When I climbed the steps into the bus the driver said it was full and I'd have to wait until the next bus. I explained that I had signed out of my dorm and I was anxious to go home for the holidays.

"I counted as they got on, Miss, and all the seats is full," the driver said.

"I'll just sit here on the step," I said and sat down.

"Look," the driver said, "I'm late as it is so I can't fiddle with you no more."

"Never mind," I said, sitting on the top step without turning to look at the driver. "I'll be fine."

The driver started to get up. Checking his watch, he muttered something, sat down and closed the door. The driver jerked the transmission into reverse and backed the bus out of the loading dock heading for the highway north.

The step was a hard place to sit and I soon realized there was a cold draft coming through under the door. My butt was going to be frozen stiff shortly and I was thinking maybe I should have tried to get the next bus in the morning. It was going to be a tough 26 hours.

We were about a half hour into the trip and my butt was frozen solid when a small, black woman came to the front of the bus. I glanced down the aisle and saw she was holding on to each seat back as the bus rocked down the highway. I thought she was going to talk to the driver but instead she looked down and tapped me on the shoulder.

"Miss," she said, trying to overcome the noise of the highway bleeding through the door, "you can have my seat; it's on the left near the back."

I turned and looked up into the face of a little black woman possibly three times my age. She wore a tattered tan scarf and held two small cloth bags in her arms.

"No, I'm fine," I lied. "You go ahead and sit back down."

As I leaned back to talk to her I had looked down the length of the bus to see that most of the passengers were watching the proceedings. That was the first I had a chance to notice that, except for me, all of the passengers on the bus, as well as the driver, were black. This was a first for me. I was the only Caucasian in a bus of blacks and it gave me a funny feeling. I smiled a nervous smile and nodded to those leaning out into the aisle. At that moment I wanted to fit in. I wanted to be black. Was this how they felt most of the time in our country?

"No, miss," the woman said with a crinkle around her eyes, "you need to move to my seat and I will sit on the step."

I pulled my jacket tighter around me and assured her again that I was fine.

"Miss," she kneeled down next to me and spoke quietly into my face, being careful not to fall into me, "you are entitled to a seat more than I am. It's as simple as that. It is going to be a long ride so you need to move and let me sit down, please."

The statement about privilege hurt and I stared out the narrow windows of the door at the wet highway speeding by, spraying the thin windows in the door. The rain had turned to a light snow and slush was splattering the bus as faster cars passed us. Their tail lights formed red streaks on my thin windows. When I turned back, the woman was gone.

I wrapped my arms around my knees and squeezed my eyes shut, trying to ignore what was around me and go to sleep.

"Miss, I have an idea," one of the other passengers said, tapping me on the shoulder as he kneeled down on one knee. This time it was a large man in worn jeans and a brown jacket. "Most of us are going to New York for the holiday and a seat won't open soon. It's going to be a long ride sitting on that hard step."

"Thanks, but I'm okay," I said looking up, wanting to take a low profile, unconsciously covering my pale white hands. Why did they have to make a big deal out of my stupidity for arriving late at the bus station? I wasn't hurting anybody sitting there wrapped in a ball with my frozen butt and my jacket pulled tightly around me.

"Look, we're in this together," he said. "Are you nervous about being on the bus with us?"

"No," I said, "I'm doing okay up here."

"Miss, if we all take an hour on the step it won't be too hard on any of us and we'll all get to where we are going."

Well, the more I protested, the more he insisted. He also had another offer to make, one that made the trip special to me to this day.

I finally agreed to move to his seat and he sat on the step. Every hour after that each of the passengers took an hour's turn on the step. At the suggestion of the man in the brown coat, each time one of the passengers moved to the front I moved to their seat. This checkers game at 70 miles an hour allowed me to meet each of the passengers in the bus. For nearly 24 hours I talked, read and sometimes dozed with each of the riders. I learned their family stories, their work, their worst fears and their dreams and they learned mine. I don't remember all of the stories but I'll never forget their smiles and their kindness that day and night on a northbound bus.

We had a long way to go in this country to heal from the loss of our president and to reach equality for all. Likewise, I had a long way to go with my education in and out of class. Nonetheless, I had received a master's degree in one semester at school in the problems and directions we needed to take in the country; more importantly, the direction I should take. It was a ride to remember.

Author's Note: A word of thanks for this story goes to a special friend and neighbor in Naples, Florida. This is a fictionalized version of a real story she experienced during her college days at the height of the civil rights movement.

Downsizing Dan

By Steven R. Roberts

What the hell just happened?

Dan was sitting in his office chair staring out his dirty office window at the brick wall of the next building 10 feet away. It's a good thing the windows couldn't be opened. It didn't make sense, no matter how you looked at it. Daniel Reed, 51, had just been let go, downsized, early retired and fired. It didn't matter what you called it, his mediocre career had been ambushed and he was unemployed.

Ten minutes earlier Dan had reported to the boss's office just as Tom Rexal, one of the other buyers, walked out. Tom's face showed no expression one way or the other.

All 18 of the employees in the purchasing department were scheduled to meet with their supervisor, Rick Adams, to talk about their careers and the state of the company. Russell Metals Manufacturing was in trouble. Russell's customers were struggling against foreign competition, and orders of Russell's assemblies were off nearly 25 percent in the past two years. There had been a round of downsizing six months earlier and three of the department's employees had been let go. Dan survived but he actually wasn't surprised. He was dependable, punctual and loyal. Yes, that's what he was. Nobody had ever questioned the quality or volume of his work. He wasn't exactly flashy or as smooth as his bosses, but the work got done even though he had been handling two jobs since the last round of layoffs.

"Dan, come in. Have a seat," Tom said. "You know Ron Pizzimenti from Personnel." Dan nodded and sat down across the conference table from the two men.

"Dan, as you know, the overseas guys are eating our lunch. Our market share is in the toilet and frankly we're being forced to reduce costs and resize the company to compete. Ron is going to explain the actions we're taking today."

That was it. Six minutes of scripted bullshit later, Dan shook hands with both men and walked out of the office, passing Frank Hidemos, another buyer who was on the way in to see the boss. Suddenly one of the company's best employees was unemployed. Pizzimenti actually had the nerve to say he'd have to turn in his security badge on the spot and clean out his desk by the end of the day. The company had been known to escort an employee off the premises if he or she had committed a crime against the firm. Apparently, downsized losers were being given to the end of the day to pack.

Back in his cubicle, Dan sat looking out his window, consumed with anger and disappointment. The company must be run by total idiots, by full-goose clowns, he thought.

How could he be one of the three to go on this round? Who were the other two? He had better not find out Loni had been retained while he had been let go. She was a joke. She didn't even understand business dress. Besides, she had a nervous giggle when negotiations got tense with suppliers. Buying veterans knew there was a time to state your final offer and then shut up and let the awkward tension build. Just at the wrong time Loni had a tendency to giggle and break the spell.

Dan scanned the three framed pictures sitting on the edge of his desk. What was he going to tell Nancy? He had made a big deal with their kids, Billy and little Sophie, that hard work and focus paid off. He had said it too many times. Where did that leave him now?

He looked down at his schedule for the day. He was supposed to meet later in the morning with a supplier and after that with an engineering committee. Dan would get through both meetings ahead of the news in his usual quietly confident style.

Grace stuck her head around the door. She was the buyer in the next cubicle and they covered for each other during vacations. "Hey Dan, you survive?"

"Yea, how about you?" Dan said. He was startled by her direct question and he lied without thinking. The denial surprised him and belied his normal truthful approach. As soon as it was out he wished he hadn't said it.

"Somehow I made it," Grace said with false modesty. She was actually one of the brighter stars in the department. "I heard Tom got the axe and that bozo in supplier liaison, what's his name, Kevin. I'm not sure about the others. Anyway, glad to see that my buddy-buyer made it." Grace's phone rang and just as quickly as she had poked her head in, she was gone.

Surely, Rick knew who was carrying the load after all of the company's layoffs. It occurred to Dan that maybe Rick hadn't made the decision as to who would be let go. Maybe their manager, D.J. Berger, had picked the losers. But, if Rick had made the choices the whole event was that much more devastating.

Berger, a Harvard grad who had never been seen without his suit coat, didn't come into Rick's department often but when he did he seemed disinterested. He would walk with his head down and go directly into Rick Adam's office, closing the door. There were a couple of stories floating around indicating Berger loosened up when he had a few drinks. A couple of months earlier Dan had seen Berger at a Tigers baseball game. Nancy was visiting the restroom as Dan checked out the crowd and the game with his small binoculars. From his seat in the upper deck he could see the company box. He noticed that Berger and Rick Adams were entertaining guests along with a gathering of buyers and a couple of people Dan didn't recognize. Dan had been to the box earlier in the season and he knew there would be considerable drinking as the game progressed. He'd said his hellos that night at the game, had a beer, and left in the sixth inning.

Dan swiveled in his office chair and wondered if he would be able to buy the chair for the house. At the same time he wondered if they could keep the house. He and Nancy had fallen in love with the house on Church Street before they knew the price. Dan's negotiating skills had made little impact on the selling price, but he had agreed to the purchase since Nancy was already planning the furniture for each room. It was a bit of a stretch but Dan was sure they'd be OK considering his pay and the pay raises scheduled for September each year.

The Tigers game had been a blowout the evening Dan and Nancy attended. The Yankees were ahead seven runs to one by the fifth inning and the visitors scored two more in the eighth. Understandably, waves of locals started for the gates and the place was nearly half empty by the ninth. Dan and Nancy stayed to take in the game and the fireworks that followed on Friday nights. In the meantime they could see the lights of the city skyline and the moon glimmering in the surface of the Detroit River.

Dan had been a little surprised that the party in the company box had ended early and it was empty. The box was dark behind the tinted-glass sliding doors, and even the lights from the game provided no light to the interior of the box.

The game ended 9 to 1 and the dedicated few awaited the traditional fireworks display. Nancy put on her jacket around 10 pm as the pyrotechnic afterglow lit up the sky. The remaining kids and an occasional drunk gave their accompanying "oohs" and "aahs" to each rocket and color burst. Dan swung his binoculars around, scanning the jubilant crowd, and his gaze landed on the company box just as one of the explosions illuminated the sky and the box below. As Dan looked down into the box he could see a couple on the couch. It was clear that the girl was the buyer, Loni. Dan recognized the yellow sundress, the same inappropriate thing she'd worn to work that day. With the next burst of fireworks Dan could see the spaghetti straps were down around Loni's waist along with the top of the dress. The man's shirttail was out and he was facing Loni so Dan couldn't see his face.

Another rocket revealed more of the same scene. Then a burst lit the box like noon and the man turned and looked skyward shielding his eyes. The man was his boss's boss, D.J. Berger. The couple was standing now and the next flash of light revealed the yellow dress dropping slowly to the floor. Berger had taken off his shirt and Loni was struggling to loosen his belt. The finale of the fireworks included several white flash bombs and the couple seemed to sense they were not hidden by the tinted booth sliding doors. The following light burst in the sky showed the couple reassembling their clothing and gathering themselves, making for the door. Berger slipped on his suit coat and combed his hair, then they were gone.

"Oh Dan, look at the finale," Nancy said, not noticing that Dan was looking elsewhere. "It's great to see the city alive at this hour of the night."

"Beautiful," Dan said, "absolutely beautiful."

Dan opened a desk drawer and saw nothing much worth packing - 11 assorted ball point pens, three or four working, a ruler with a supplier's name on it and a roll of breath mints. His cost-savings Buyer-of-the-Year plaque from five years ago was lying in the dust at the bottom of the drawer. There was a coffee mug, a personal file and the three framed pictures. Somehow it seemed there should be some important stuff, after 14 years, but there just wasn't.

What were the prospects of another job? The papers had reported layoffs and early retirements of tens of thousands in the area in the previous three years. Joining that long line of job seekers made Dan tired just to think of it. Younger people networked when they were between jobs. They told everybody and his brother they needed a job. Dan's generation hid in a cave until a plan was developed or until luck landed in the opening of the cave. It was hard to clear his mind enough to see any real options. He needed to get into his cave and think.

Toward the end of the day, Dan sat with his head down on the desk. The phone rang five times during the late afternoon but he let the calls go to voice mail. He had always been slow to anger, and he had no real experience with rage. Would anger and rage do any good in this situation? Did he want to be someplace where they said they didn't want him? On the other hand this job was a good part of how he kept score in his life.

He thought of several options. He could start a business of his own if he could think of a business he could afford to start. He could stand in line at one of those job fairs. He could ask Nancy's uncle, Reed, for a job at the brewery over in Ludington. He could write a letter to the company's president, Jonathon Russell.

After thinking about it for a while Dan realized there was only one idea that might actually give him a chance to reach his goal. The question was whether it was beneath him. It certainly employed his negotiating skills finely honed in his work. He sat up straight in his chair. No, it wasn't beneath him. In fact it was simply another contract negotiation. Dan needed the job for more reasons than he had time to count. Since Pizzamenti had taken his security badge, he had to make it work before he left the building.

"Hi, hon," Dan said, calling home. "You alright?"

"Sure, Dan," Nancy said. "Hon, on your way home could you pick up a dozen corn on the cob?"

"Okay, I got it," Dan said. "Oh, I'll be 30 minutes late tonight. I've got an important project here and I need a few minutes to finish."

"Rick, got a minute?" Dan said, walking into his boss's office, closing the door and sitting across the desk.

"What's up, Dan?" Rick said standing and slipping a handful of files into his briefcase. "I was just on my way out."

"This won't take a minute," Dan said. "Rick, I'm convinced you didn't have the main say on my dismissal this morning but frankly I don't really want to know. Whatever the case, I'm going to get my job back and I've decided you are going to help me." Rick was frowning and paying attention but he didn't try to say anything. He sat his briefcase on the floor and sat down at his desk.

"Dan, downsizing is tough on all of us and I'm really sorry that..."

"Rick, you probably know Berger has been sleeping with Loni," Dan said. "I think this is the likely reason I got the axe today instead of her." Dan was guessing that Berger's relationship with Loni had progressed beyond the groping stage since the Tiger's game.

"Dan, you can't make accusations like that," Rick said. "My God, that kind of stupidity could get you fired." Dan smiled at the irony.

"Rick, I'm going to get my job back before I go home tonight and either you meet with Berger or I will. I've got multiple witnesses that have seen him with Loni, sometimes in compromising situations." Dan had no witnesses other than himself, but such overstatements were standard negotiating hyperbole.

"And Rick," Dan was standing looking down at his boss, "in case Berger denies the Loni thing," Dan paused, "remind him that several of us know about the supplier who painted his house and the one who laid the new driveway last summer up at his cottage. I'm sure Mr. Russell would be more than interested in this information."

"Dan, I suggest that you get out of here," Rick said speaking through closed teeth, "You have been instructed to clear your things and be out of here by five o'clock. You are no longer authorized to be in this building so don't let the door hit you in the ass when you leave."

This outburst was also standard negotiating technique, Dan thought, as he turned to leave Rick's office. He returned to his cubicle, picked up the Journal and put his feet up on his desk.

Somewhere around 5:25 pm Rick walked into Dan's office and sat in the visitor chair. Rick didn't say anything. He looked sideways at the wall, subconsciously clicking his ballpoint pen as he did when negotiations got serious. Rick had on his negotiating face but his normally smooth demeanor was missing and his jowly face was sagging more than usual. He stood and circled the chair, holding onto the back with both hands.

Dan looked up without expression.

"I talked to D.J. I insisted that I needed more veterans on the team to make the cost cutting objectives for the department. I also told him you were our best negotiator. Anyway, D.J. agreed to revise our personnel plans. Here, you can use my security badge to get in tomorrow morning."

"Good negotiation Boss," Dan said, looking Rick in the eyes. "I assume I can expect a little extra in the annual raise in September, me being the best negotiator you got in the department."

"Goodnight Dan," Rick said, firming his jaw and turning a shade of red as he walked down the hall toward the parking lot.

Dan didn't say anything as the boss made his exit. He just leaned back in his chair, looked out his window and smiled at the brick wall. It was time to go home for dinner.

THE BOXING OF SEAN

By Carl Steinhouse

You've heard about "Abie's Irish Rose." This story is more like Rose's Irish Sean.

When they were young, Sean O'Hara swept Rose Finkelstein off her feet. Mama would have killed her if Rose told her she wanted to marry out of her religion, much less an Irishman who, Mama said, "all drank too much." So Rose and Sean eloped, and Mama, when she found out, sat *shiva*, mourning the "death" of her daughter—to Mama, Rose no longer existed. Mothers could be like that sometimes. But it didn't last long. Mama milked the drama for all it was worth, but eventually resurrected Rose because she loved her too much.

For a few years, love and infatuation sustained their relationship. Rose tolerated Sean's drinking—Mama was right, after all—and Sean tolerated Rose's Jewish friends and Jewish customs.

As the bloom wore off the rose—so to speak—they co-existed under an armed truce. He could drink as long as he didn't knock her around. And she could enjoy her friends as long as she didn't insist on his participation.

Traveling was the one thing they enjoyed doing together. They went on safaris, cruised down the Amazon, snorkeled at the Great Barrier Reef, explored the Taj Mahal, and covered most of Europe.

Rose tried to keep Sean on a healthy diet--low fat meat, fish, salads, and the like. But it was hopeless. On his own with his buddies, he enjoyed bacon and eggs cooked in lard (like his mother used to make them), pork rinds (his father's favorite), pig's feet (like he ate at Aunt Maureen's), and whipped cream desserts—well, you get the picture. Rose finally gave up the losing battle and he simply ate what he wanted—garbage in Rose's opinion—not that Sean cared one whit what she thought.

Where their armed truce broke down was over money. Sean made a good living as a manufacturer's rep, selling Irish linens to wholesalers and retailers in the east and mid-west. But he was stingy with a capital "S". They had two children—Michael, who was bar mitzvahed, and Jenny, who was baptized—I guess it was a compromise worked out in heaven.

Sean resented that Rose didn't pull her weight by working to bring in money. "Bringing up your children is a full time job," she would yell at him. She always called them "his" children when they fought.

"Besides," she added, "you wouldn't pay for a college education for me. So, I ask you, *schmuck*"—Sean understood THAT Yiddish word—"just what am I trained to do? I'll tell you. *Bubkes*, nothing, that's what!"

Even in the area of their mutual love, travel, they fought over money. He always wanted to go on the cheap—cheap tours, cheap hotels and Big Macs when he could find them. He'd never buy travel insurance and his penurious tipping embarrassed her. But they worked through it. She ate some meals in medium-priced restaurants and he ate in pubs and taverns and the like.

Their final trip together was to be to Ireland, London, Paris and three other European capitals. Sean was definitely showing his age. The years of abuse he inflicted on his body took its toll. The handsome young man of Rose's youth was now a slob--a pot-bellied, jowled and bald wreck--with liver spots. He already had two heart by-pass operations. But to tell you the truth, Rose wasn't a bargain any more, either. Her breasts, stomach and behind had dropped, her golden locks of hair were now dirty gray wisps—and she had varicose veins like a river delta.

Still, she enjoyed having sex—she really had to like it to do it with a fat blob like Sean. But Sean wasn't particularly interested in sex anymore. It took quite a bit of cajoling and challenging of his manhood by Rose to get him going. Believe me, it was work to build him up three or four times a year.

Anyway, Rose and Sean were in Ireland on the first leg of the budget tour, the cheapest Rose could find so he wouldn't raise a fuss.

On their second night in Dublin, Rose got the urge—badly. She cajoled, rubbed, cooed and challenged Sean—the whole *schmear*. He sighed. They had gotten in early, he hadn't drank much and there had been a three-month hiatus, so he figured he was out of excuses—the headache one only worked for Rose. He decided he'd better capitulate if he wanted any peace for the next few days.

"Okay, Rose, okay, just button it up."

Rose smiled—he just had to get in a last retort to save his dignity.

Once they started the process of having sex, she was a wild woman who could get even Sean to the point where he actually wanted to do it.

When Sean reached that point of no return in that Irish hotel room, she whispered in his ear, blowing in it at the same time, "Do it standing up!"

"What?"

"Just like Jack Nicholson in 'Five Easy Pieces,' when he did the girl running around the room."

"What?"

"You heard me, my hero."

He shrugged. He shouldn't have been surprised. She often gravitated to the wild side when she got excited. They once did it in the men's john in Giovanni's Italian Restaurant--in the toilet stall, no less. Another time it was in the fitting room in the gentlemen's suit department at Macy's. Of course, they were much younger then and didn't need a lot of preliminaries.

He wished Rose would just grow up. When she got it in her mind to go kinky, there was no dissuading her.

"Ugh," he grunted, "it's not so easy anymore, Rose."

"You can do it, my big strong Adonis," she panted.

Once around the hotel room, bumping into the dresser, nightstand and chair, and Sean had had it—and I really mean had it—big time. He came crashing down on Rose, pinning her to the floor, almost crushing her.

"Sean," she gasped, "enough already, you're suffocating me to death!"

No reaction.

"Sean!" she said sharply.

No answer.

It took her several minutes to extricate herself from underneath his 240-pound frame.

She slapped his face.

No reaction--nothing. He was ashen gray.

She knew—he was stone dead.

She moaned.

What to do? She thought.

First things first. She got dressed.

"*Oy*, the embarrassment—if the tour knew what we were doing when he *plotzed*."

With great difficulty, she put on his jockey shorts. Too late, she realized the fly was in the back. She shook her head--it'll have to be, I don't have the *kishkes* to change it. It was bad enough she had to struggle to get on his pants and shirt.

Sean was carted away. The autopsy revealed he died of a massive coronary. The Irish coroner was a very nice person--he didn't say anything about the strange reversal of Sean's underwear.

All the members of the tour were very sympathetic.

"What a tragedy," one member moaned. They all nodded. So Rose nodded.

Many asked, "Is there anything I can do for you?" But they really didn't mean it, Rose knew. After all, they were on vacation, weren't they?

Some of the men volunteered to go to synagogue, others to church to say a prayer for Sean. But Rose sensed it was out of courtesy and not any burning desire to take the time to put in a good word for Sean's eternal soul.

Rose shook her head, "It's not necessary, the priest gave him last rites at the hospital—he's well covered."

They nodded, relieved that they wouldn't miss the tour to the Waterford glass factory and store, where, the tour guide reported, there were good buys.

The tour director, always prepared, had a list of funeral parlors in Dublin—Rose picked one—Finnegan's Fine Funerals. She always had a thing for alliterations.

Director Finnegan, in his most sonorous voice—you know how funeral directors can be—"Madame O'Hara, please accept our deepest sympathies for your loss."

She nodded, non-committally, tired already of all the sympathy from strangers. She was more interested now in the damages.

"We can arrange for the Madame, to send you and Mr. O'Hara home on Air Lingus, on tomorrow morning's flight."

"How much?"

"Excuse me?"

She got annoyed, the question was clear enough. "How much will it cost to fly back?"

"Ah, of course. About $5,000."

She blinked. "Just great," she said. "The cheap bastard refused to buy trip insurance."

His eyes widened. He shrugged.

She took out her tour itinerary and scanned it. Then she smiled.

"Can you fit him in a small box?"

He looked quizzically, spreading out his arms. "Madame, he is a big man. It will be very difficult."

"Do whatever you have to do to fit him in a small box, but don't tell me how you do it."

He sighed. "Very well, Madame."

"Can you treat the body so it will last a few weeks?"

"Of course, Madame. We at Finnegan's Finest Funerals are the best in the business. We can embalm Mr. O'Hara to last for a year, if necessary."

"The three-week special will be sufficient, thank you."

"And then, Madame?"

"And then, deliver Mr. O'Hara to Heathrow Airport, BA flight 89 to Paris on October 4th, 9 o'clock in the morning."

"Excuse me?"

"Mr. O'Hara will be my luggage. We paid for this trip and we will, so help me, take it to every damn city on the tour."

"I understand." But he really didn't.

Members of the tour were surprised when Rose showed up at the bus for the day's events. She was not going to miss another day.

"Rose," the tour director said, "you can't go. What are you going to do with Sean?"

"What else? We paid for the tour, and unless you give me a full refund now, we're going."

"You know there's no refund once the tour starts."

"I know, therefore, we are going."

"Rose, we can't take Sean with us, he's dead."

"And just why not? He's my luggage—if he's over the weight limit, I'll pay the extra charges."

"But he's dead, Rose."

"Good, he'll be the one member who won't complain or *kvetch*."

The tour guide couldn't match Rose's logic. He stopped trying.

Rose threw out Sean's clothes and their luggage. She packed only the clothes she could fit in her carry-on.

The tour group, and Sean in his box, visited Paris, Vienna, Budapest and Prague. Rose had a wonderful time.

She handled the local authorities with aplomb as she overcame all their bureaucratic objections about letting Sean into the country. They were no match for her so they impounded the uncomplaining Sean at the airport and delivered him to Rose's next flight. That made things infinitely easier for her.

Rose arrived home with Sean, a well-to-do widow.

She spared no expense giving Sean the finest Irish wake ever seen in the Queens, New York, community. She, of course, didn't open Sean's box for the wake because she wasn't sure he was in one piece. I suppose a lot of people wondered how Sean fit into such a small box. None were so impolitic as to ask. But nobody seemed to mind; they were enjoying the fabulous spread, even if it was somewhat unusual for a wake—lox and bagels, white fish, baked salmon spread, chopped liver, Hebrew National salami, ruggalah, etc.—catered by the local Jewish deli. And, of course, there was plenty of the finest Irish whiskey.

Guest Author Bio: Carl Steinhouse, a retired lawyer, was a former federal prosecutor for the United States Department of Justice and thereafter, in private practice specializing in class actions, white-collar crime, civil and criminal trials and investigation. He served in the U.S. Army Counterintelligence Corps during the Korean War. He has published six books on the Holocaust.

El Stupido and the Blue Pajamas

By Steven R. Roberts

Day Two:

The minute the mirror fell off and shattered on the interstate, I knew I was doomed. The right side mirror on my rented Ryder truck had been shaking the previous day to the point that I did my best to travel in the right hand lane all day. The one time I joined another interstate highway in the outer lane it had taken me 10 miles and several quick reactions to blaring horns before I trusted the shaky mirror enough to make my way back to the right lane. That night at the motel, I jammed a folded match book cover behind the mirror to hold it in place. The next morning, in the St. Louis rush hour, the mirror was steady, but now it was showing me the side of my truck. When we were stopped in the morning traffic, I jumped across the cab, knocked Bingo into his litter box on the floor, and adjusted the mirror.

"Good morning El Stupido, come in please," said daughter, Maggie.

"Morning Blue Pajamas. Steady as she goes today." Each vehicle was equipped with one of the cheap walkie-talkies I had purchased at K-Mart so we could keep in touch during the trip. The limited range of the toy-like devices made it necessary to be no more than 100 feet apart on the highway. There were a few cell phones around in those summer days of 1993 but we didn't own any.

My wife, Sonja, and I were driving our daughter, Maggie, from Michigan to the University of Texas in Austin. The six-wheel rental truck was full of the furniture, clothing, a TV and a bicycle that Maggie had accumulated living on her own for three years after undergrad school. Our daughter had surprised her mother and me by announcing a year earlier that she wanted to get an MBA. She was quite clear on the choice of a school.

"I want a school south of the Mason Dixon line," she said. "I've seen all of the snow and ice I want to see in my life." Sonja and I absorbed the fact that our daughter's view of the right climate for grad school would undoubtedly carry over to her choice for living afterwards.

"El Capitan here," I said, holding the red button, "come in Blue Pajamas." I had started the trip the previous morning as "El Capitan" and my wife and daughter had named themselves "Blue Pajamas." I had made a few minor driving errors the first day and the ladies decided to rename me "El Stupido," without asking for my vote. My nerves were too raw to appreciate the joke. I might be pot-bellied and balding, but damn it I was still the provider, the husband, the dad. I was also annoyed that our daughter had once again chosen to go out of state to college. What a waste of money. Maggie could talk her mother into anything, including wasting our money. Sonja and I didn't have any college, both having worked right out of high school. Now our daughter had to have two colleges, both at out-of-state fees.

Anyway, that's how we ended up in a two-vehicle convoy from our Detroit suburb to Austin in the heat of August, 1993.

Day One:

Within seconds of starting the trip early the day before, there was an initial blast over the airwaves.

"El Capitan, El Capitan!" Maggie said, holding in the talk button. It was the first of many messages during the trip commenting on the truck driver's performance. In my driver's side mirror I could see Maggie and her mother moving away from the curb following me in Maggie's four-year-old Escort.

"What happened?" I asked starting forward, working my way through the gears.

"El Capitan, you just backed over the Miller's trash cans," Maggie said. "The cans are flat. There are papers and garbage blowing all over their yard."

"Bingo and I are on the road, Blue Pajamas," I said. "Let's not get tied up in a neighborhood squabble. It serves them right for running over your bike when you were eight. Don't you remember? Let's face it, Maggie, Bingo and I are truckers now, and due to the nature of our work, there may be collateral damage. Catch us if you can."

With that, the two vehicles pulled out of our neighborhood at daybreak and we were on the road. Twenty minutes later we were hauling west on I-94, acting like we knew what we were doing. Bingo had done a quick check of the periphery of the truck cab and was busy giving himself a thorough bath in the passenger's seat. I was focused on staying in my lane. This truck was just a big pickup I kept telling myself but it felt scary, like any minute it could decide to run off the road and flip on its side. For one thing, I could only see the cars around me and back of me on the highway by relying on my mirrors.

"El Capitan, this is Blue PJs. Isn't it a lovely day for a trip?" Maggie asked, knowing that I was uneasy in my seat.

"Blue PJs, I'll have you know Bingo is so relaxed with my driving that he has finished bathing and is upside down asleep on the passenger's seat."

"El Capitan, please keep your eyes on the road," Sonja said. "Gary, even from back here, I can tell when you are talking to Bingo. It's the same when we are together and you turn to talk to me. That's when you cross the lane lines. Remember what the race car drivers say. 'The car goes where the eyes go.'"

"Yes, dear," I said. Letting up on the talk button, I added, "Bingo, I need to practice my no-look repartee."

Shortly after passing Jackson, we turned on I-69 toward Ft. Wayne, Indiana. During day one my attitude would move gradually from being mad about the waste of time driving to Texas, to scared as hell I would run off the road. I was trying to get to the quietly confident stage which seemed elusive.

"I think I can do this, Bingo," I said. "What do you think?" A black-eyed all-knowing glance came in return. Bingo spread out on his back, in the passenger seat, lacking any modesty, and dozed off again. The cat was a three-year-old, long-haired, tabby-colored extra expense and he was supposed to be keeping me awake. Instead he was doing the opposite. For sure he was no conversationalist.

I had never realized how much a trucker's life is dependent on truthful mirrors. Were there lying mirrors, I wondered? It was possible.

How else could you explain those mirrors in the Cedar Point Fun House?

I was used to actually seeing the vehicles around me. Now, I had to see other vehicles and judge the speed, angle of approach and impending merging of sheet-metal based on reflections. I had been a supervisor in an ACO warehouse out on I-275 for nine years, but I had never driven anything bigger than those times I'd moved a lift truck out of the way. At 49, my mind and body were not enthused about new things like the finer points of truck highway etiquette.

When I was learning how to drive the truck, the Ryder guys told me to hold my hands at 10 o'clock and 2 o'clock on the steering wheel. I was to keep the white line between my thumb and forefinger of my left hand. My guiding thumb allowed me to minimize the honking. Well, there was the exception when I swerved to the left one whole lane as Bingo threw up a hairball mid-afternoon.

"Mayday! Mayday! Blue PJs," I shouted, holding down the button.

"El Stupido, you can't say that word on the airwaves," Maggie said. I could hear Sonja in the background swearing in Spanish.

"Blue PJs, I'd like to know what you would say if Bingo puked up a slimy baseball in your lap." I said, trying to drive and reach for the handkerchief in my back pocket.

"El Stupido, it's just that you can't say that word unless the truck is in the river."

"Blue PJs, I'm not allowed to say hairball?" I asked, holding down the button. "You'd say mayday, too, if you had this putrid gunk in your lap." I pushed Bingo aside, did a no-look grab with the handkerchief, and threw the baseball out my window. The wind threw the glob back against the door of the truck and I white knuckled the truck toward St. Louis.

"Dad, a piece of green slime just hit my windshield. You can't throw stuff out the window," Maggie said. "There are fines for littering, you know."

"Sorry, Maggie," I said. "Turn on your wipers."

"I did," Maggie said. "Your dirty handkerchief got stuck to my wiper and smeared the mess all over my windshield."

After a full day of fighting the red-button audits from the Escort, unsympathetic traffic, inadequate road signage, gummy fur balls and idiot drivers presenting symphonies written-for-horns every time I crept slightly into the next lane, I made another alleged leadership mistake.

"El Stupido, this is Blue PJs. What are you doing?" Maggie asked, just after eight in the evening as she saw me getting over to the exit lane. "We can't stop here."

"Blue PJs, why not?" I asked. "Bingo is exhausted from a busy day of hissing at me as well as all the work involved with sleeping, eating, pooping, peeing and puking. We're all tired and I've had it trying to manhandle this six-wheeled beast all day," I said. "I can't face St. Louis tonight."

"St. Louis will be three times as big and busy in the morning," Maggie said.

"Honey, we don't want Dad dozing off and driving into the river, do we?" Sonja asked, with an exhausted sigh. "The Mississippi is coming up and I don't want Dad to have a chance to use the Mayday word legitimately."

Day Two (continued):

"Well, Bingo, you might know, Maggie was right. Look at this mess," I said, as we resumed our trek on I-70 the second morning. Approaching St. Louis in the freeway northern loop, we alternated between speeds of zero and 45 mph while Bingo ate his breakfast, peed in the litter box, stretched and went back to his well deserved nap in the passenger's seat.

"For God's sake, Bingo, you just got up," I said, giving the cat a glance and stroking his ears back against his streaked caramel and white face.

Traffic was bumper to bumper encouraging the girls to continue their audit of my driving. It seemed there wasn't much I was doing right. Knowing our next important exit, at I-44, was coming in five or six miles, I checked both mirrors to make sure the red Escort was in sight. They had been there last time I looked. Damn it, where were they? I had no choice but to keep going. They could certainly maneuver that little car around in this traffic better than I could handle this stupid truck.

"Blue Pajamas, this is El Capitan. Come in please."

"Blue Pajamas, do you read me?" I asked, looking at the toy walkie-talkie as if a picture of the two ladies might appear on the receiver.

"Hey, where the hell are you girls?" I shouted, just as I noticed the line of cars in my lane was stopped.

I stood on the brakes, throwing Bingo into his litter box and spreading his food and water over the floor of the cab. When we started up again two important things happened. I jerked through the gears and checked the right side mirror just in time to see it come loose and fall, shattering on the road. Drivers in the next lane swerved at the sound of seven years of bad luck. The second happening was that I realized Bingo and I had missed the exit onto westbound I-44.

"Damn it, Bingo, how can one driving team have so much bad luck?"

I couldn't see the right lane so I proceeded down the I-270 ring road until I could speed past a slower vehicle and take a chance on swerving blind to the right lane. I exited at the town of Mattersnut.

"Can you give me directions to the local Ryder rental business?" I asked the old guy at the gas station. Pushing his straggly gray hair behind his ears and resetting his worn hat, he looked through his wire rimmed glasses at my truck then at me.

"I need a new part or a new truck before I get back on the highway," I added. "You got any vanity mirrors?"

"Not a big call for that kind-a thing here, this bein' a truck stop and all," the old man said. "I got lots a truck parts in the back." I could just make out the name, Jake, through the grease on his overalls.

We walked down the aisles of the store past everything from milk to beer to shaving cream and condoms.

"Jake," I said, "I'm sort of in a hurry."

"I bin pickin' up parts that's been fallen off trucks 'round here for 25 years," Jake said, wiping his hands on a greasy rag that was doing more harm than good. "I'm 'bout sure I'd have what ya need, course lessin I don't."

"How far is the Ryder store?" I asked again.

"Nearest one I ever heard of is up in the big city and that's a ways."

"You got a breakfast place around here?" I asked.

"Yep, there's Maryanne's 'round the curve in the road," Jake said, wiping his hands again.

"How far is that?"

"Oh, I'd say it's 'bout hollarin' distance."

I turned to leave.

"Tell Maryanne I'll be 'round in an hour," Jake said with a twinkle in his eyes.

"You got a menu?" I asked, sitting at the counter at Maryanne's.

"We had one but it got stolen couple weeks back," Maryanne said. "The way it works round here at this hour of the morning is that you let me know what you want and I'll see what I got back there."

"You don't mind my cat, do you?" I asked.

"No, I'm okay but ya better hope my dog, Elvis, don't get wind of the little puff."

"Is Elvis in the building?" I asked.

"He's asleep in the kitchen," she said. "He sleeps in front of the fryer most days. He likes to lick the grease off the floor."

After breakfast I walked back to the gas station.

"Where you headed?" Jake asked, replenishing the beer jerky display.

"I'm taking my daughter's furniture to Texas. My wife and daughter are following me in a car," I said.

"They're following you?" Jake turned looking out at the parking lot.

"Well, they were. We got separated and they're ahead of me now, probably up on I-44 going west."

"What about this?" Jake asked, picking up an item off the counter and looking at himself in the mirrored surfaces.

"Those are sunglasses," I said, not sure if he was kidding. "I don't want to look like a highway patrolman."

"Come on," Jake said, grabbing a roll of duct tape and walking out to the truck. "Partner, this will have to do if you're goin' to have a chance of catchin' your family up on 44."

"Put your finger right here," he said.

I held the glasses in place and he bent the temples around the mirror frame. Jake adjusted the glasses as I sat behind the wheel and gave him instructions. Finally, I could see the road beside the truck in one of the lenses so we were good to go. My world of knowledge about what was happening on the right side was suddenly limited to two mirrors the size of eggs. Of course it was better than the previous system, which consisted of moving to the right until I heard an angry horn or the sound of scraping sheet metal.

"You better hurry if you goin' a lead them, partner," Jake said, wiping my fender with his rag. "Tell ya what. You can take 40 miles off the trip if you just stay on old route 50, headin' west. You can join the interstate and maybe catch 'em from there. Take this road and turn right at the white farm house with the slanted porch."

Back on the road, Bingo and I were a little tense. It was an overcast day with the wind swaying my rig side to side. The main trouble was that we were off of any of the trip tics I had obtained from AAA. Proceeding through the back country, a dark storm cloud blocked the sun and I regretted having seen the movie "Deliverance" twice. There was only one lane each direction so I couldn't tell how the cop glasses were going to work out on the freeway.

"Bingo, where did Jake say this road would intersect I-44? These rural Missouri roads all look the same. Damn it, Bingo, wake up. All hands on deck."

I turned on the radio and fiddled for a station. Wouldn't you know Dan Fogelberg came on singing *Same Old Lang Syne*?

"Met my old lover at the grocery shop."

I sang, and Bingo closed his eyes. I always loved this song.

"Just for a moment I was back in school."

"Bingo, whatever happened to Carol Sue Butchi from Senior High? I heard she moved somewhere out in Iowa."

"And felt that old familiar pa-a-ain."

"Boy, don't it make you wonder where we'd be if things had worked out with Carol Sue and me? Man, she was special. Well, I guess you never knew her."

"I think dirty Jake is sacking in with Maryanne. What do you think? He's getting more than pancakes and grits back there, I can tell you that."

"If we lived out here, Bingo," I said, rubbing my traveling companion under the chin, "you could chase field mice all day long and I could sit by the river and fish, take a nap, then fish some more. You wouldn't have to be on that strict diet from the vet. By the way, mister fur ball, I saw Maryanne drop that piece of bacon under the counter for you. You were lucky Elvis didn't pick that moment to pay us a visit."

"Out here you could roam around the farm and eat what you find. I could chop wood and build a fire by the creek. I'm 49 for Christ's sake, Bingo. When is my time coming? Am I never going to be allowed to do foolish things, trek up the Rockies, ride my bike across the country, scoop up salmon in the streams up in Alaska? Bingo, tell me something. You're not married. Are you happy? Well, I suppose that's an unfair question because who the hell is? Anyhow, I think about such stuff from time to time and I just needed to bounce it off somebody, or something. Thanks for listening."

The sound of the truck's tires droned on mile after mile as we kept our own counsel for an hour or so.

"Well, I don't know about you, Bingo," I said, breaking the mood, "but the walkie-talkies were starting to get on my nerves. It's a good day to be on the road and I haven't been corrected since Mattershut. Okay little buddy, I-44 is coming up ahead and westward we will go, chasing after Thelma and Louise. Yahoo, let's go."

Out on the interstate I struggled to see in the sunglasses. If I leaned to the right, I could see along the side of my vehicle in the near lens and further to the right in the other. If another driver looked up at my mirror as he approached he might think a highway cop was staring at him in the mirror. Looking back, ol' Jake had not only saved the day with his innovation, he had invented an early version of a mirror that revealed the blind spots.

I continued diagonally down through Missouri, exiting the state at Joplin. It was raining in Oklahoma and the day was losing its light early. Traffic slowed to around 55 mph as the caravan of travelers made their way trying to do no harm. I decided I would stop early for the night in Muskogee, southeast of Oklahoma City.

Bingo was hiding from the storm when suddenly the taillights of the vehicles ahead turned the night into a red glare and the ribbon of traffic came to a sliding stop. I jammed on the brakes and tipped the truck's tail in the air. Bingo and I looked at each other in the lights from the instrument cluster. We were both thrown into the dash panel, but I managed to stop short of the car ahead of me. We took a deep breath and tried to determine if our body parts were all attached where they were supposed to be. There was a jolt as a trailing delivery van crashed into the rear of our vehicle and we heard the crash spreading glass and broken plastic parts over the highway. I cringed at the sound of collapsing sheet metal and chrome.

"Bingo, you okay?" I asked. There was no response, only the sound of approaching sirens. I reached around in the dark and found him hunkered down on the floor. I picked him up and rubbed under his chin for a minute, calling his name, but he wasn't moving. I held him on my shoulder and stepped down from the cab to check on the passengers in the van. Walking around my truck in the rain, I could see the driver still sitting behind the steering wheel.

"You okay?" I asked.

"Yea, I think so, not sure," he said, speaking in a whisper.

"I hear sirens on the way, so I think you will be checked out in a few minutes," I said. The caramel cat was a limp rag as I headed forward to check on the car ahead. The van had caused my truck to bump into the car in front of me.

I thought I could feel a heartbeat in Bingo as I walked past my open cab door. There was static coming from the cab so I stepped up to turn off the radio when I realized it wasn't turned on. The noise was coming from the console. I opened it to find the walkie-talkie crackling with static. I pushed the red button.

"Hello," I said, standing on the truck step.

"El Capitan" (static)… "El Capitan, come… please, we…"

"This is dad, is that you Maggie?"

"Daddy, …thank God you are there. Mom and I… in a giant traffic smash up and we can't..."

"I'm here honey. How is mom?"

"We're both banged up pretty bad. Mom's" (static) "on the head and her right leg is trapped under the dash. And I'm…"

"Maggie, I'm near the end of the pile up," I said, just as I heard another crash in the tailback forming behind me. "Where are you and mom?" I asked, carrying Bingo and running between the broken vehicles and dazed passengers.

"Maggie, Maggie, Sonja!"

"Daddy, we were the third car to crash, toward the front. We're both hurt and the car is in a ditch. I'm trying to wake mom up. I don't think the emergency squad is going to be able to see us down here."

"I'm coming, Maggie," I said, running, trying to keep the walkie-talkie out of the driving rain. The wind was blowing sideways and it knocked me into two dazed guys leaning against their pickup, which was minus its bumper and hood. I stumbled past seven or eight crumpled vehicles and turned toward the ditch. Running toward the Escort, I saw its nose was submerged in the drainage ditch.

"Maggie, Sonja," I said, trying to open the passenger door. Through the window the twirling red lights hit the faces of the two unconscious passengers

"Hey, down here!" I shouted to the first responders. "My wife and daughter are passed out and trapped in the vehicle."

"We're coming," shouted one of the emergency workers.

"Stand aside please, sir,"

"This is my family. They're both unconscious."

"Sir, it is much better if the trapped individuals are awake so we can be sure we are not causing additional injury."

"Maggie, Sonja!" I shouted, banging on the passenger side window.

"Sir, how did you escape from the vehicle?"

"I…"

"Stand back, sir," one of the rescue workers said, preparing to use the Jaws of Life to pry open the door.

I fell back into the side of the muddy ditch as Bingo stirred and jumped out of my arms.

"Bingo!" I shouted. The cat jumped through the slim opening made by the jaws and started licking Sonja's face. Sonja opened her eyes and screamed with fear and confusion at waking to find herself trapped and in pain. Sonja and Maggie, who had also been revived, looked in fright at the faces of strangers intermittently illuminated by flashing red lights, blowing rain, crumpled vehicles and the smell of burning rubber and leaking fluids.

An emergency worker applied the full force of the spreading device to the door and popped it open. They reached in and freed Sonja's trapped leg. She cried out as they lifted her out of the vehicle and onto a stretcher. With the driving rain washing over the scene, the workers were able to reach in and slide Maggie across the seat and place her on a stretcher. The two victims survived being carried up the muddy bank to the emergency vehicle.

"Good to go," somebody shouted, as he pushed the rear door shut and smacked it with the palm of his hand. The ambulance went to the hospital in Muskogee and Bingo and I followed a half hour later after getting my compromised, but functional, truck free from the crash scene.

Days Three, Four and Five:

Both Maggie and Sonja had concussions and Sonja had a broken ankle. I sat around the hospital for three days in between trips to the motel room to take care of the cat.

"Well, Bingo," I said, sitting on the edge of the bed in my motel room, "mom got her ankle set and both of our ladies are going to be okay. They'll be released tomorrow and we'll be on our way to Austin. You're going to have to watch your tail around her crutches."

I rolled Bingo over and scratched his chin. In gratitude he gnawed at my fingers like he hadn't eaten in a week.

"It was a bit of a wild ride for a while but we're here and, except for Sonja's ankle, we're all in one piece. Ol' Jake played a part, in his own strange way. So did the crash and so did you, old buddy. We had some good talks out on the road. I think maybe after all of this, you and I have lived enough on the wild side for a while. What do you think?"

Bingo opened his mouth and gave a hissed "Hi", which was actually the only English word the cat knew.

"I thought so."

The rental company wasn't exactly pleased when I drove in with the remains of their truck. Of course Maggie wasn't going to be happy when she finally saw her wet furniture. I figured we'd need to visit Ikea in Austin to replace some of her stuff. Sonja was uncomfortable in her cast on our way to Austin, especially since she had no place to rest it except in the litter box. Nobody was particularly pleased to be crammed into the truck cab. I still had room behind the wheel for the final day of our trip but the two ladies and Bingo were a bit grumpy, trying to share the other half of the cab.

"Bingo, could you please cover up your work in the litter box for the sanity of all of us?" I asked, without looking sideways at the others.

As soon as our daughter was settled in for school, Sonja, Bingo and I were on our way to the airport for a flight back to Detroit. I was in a collapsed sleep at 30,000 feet when my wife mentioned that our youngest boy, Michael, was going to take a new job in Seattle. I half heard her say Michael would appreciate some help in moving his stuff from Canton, Michigan, to Seattle. I kept my eyes closed as I raised my hand.

"Stewardess, could I order a drink, please?" A wide-mouthed hissing sound came from the pet carrier under my seat.

The Greatest Grandparents Up Close and Personal

By Pierette Domenica Simpson

I owe my childhood—my life—to my grandparents.

Pietro and Domenica Burzio never imagined adopting the role of parents in their mid-forties. The responsibility was thrust upon them by their daughter Vivina's unexpected pregnancy. As farmers living in a small village at the foot of the Italian Alps, Pietro and Domenica had invested hard-earned capital to assure a successful career for their daughter. She had been sent to a Catholic convent boarding school, followed by a teacher's college. As expected, my grandparents were shocked and disappointed at their 21-year-old unwed daughter's predicament.

Where could they have gone wrong, they wondered? Perhaps sequestering the young Vivina in a convent did not prepare her for the risky world of dating? As with every young woman from a small village, she yearned for a life in the big city—mostly realized by finding a big-city suitor. Vivina became smitten by a handsome, intelligent young man from Torino. Unfortunately, the magical encounter would be brief and my mother would have to turn to her parents for help to raise her child.

Pietro and Domenica willingly took on the unexpected responsibility. It became their labor of love. Vivina continued to live at home in Pranzalito, a town of 120 inhabitants. Although it was certainly not the first such pregnancy, the Catholic small-town mentality created a shameful existence, especially after she gave birth. As my mother put it,

"Raising a child alone was considered a disgrace. I felt guilty, worthless, and restless…"

In spite of the socio-economic challenges, my grandparents were determined to become co-parents.

Nonno, my grandfather, used his talents to make my wooden cradle. He raised rabbits and then used their fur to line the cradle for beauty and comfort. My nonna and mother embroidered my sheets and sewed beautiful blankets; the rough marijuana hemp cloth was difficult on the fingers, but nothing was too much effort. They prided themselves in having friends visit from neighboring towns and marvel at the most artistic and plush baby bed and bedding imaginable!

Nevertheless, my mother was unhappy being dependent; there were few jobs in post-World War II Italy. Since many townspeople were emigrating to the United States in search of higher economic rewards, Vivina made her courageous decision—to obtain a passport and passage to the New World.

Pietro and Domenica willingly accepted their new role as my surrogate parents when I was only 15 months old. After all, they loved me dearly and sacrifice was a way of life during post-war times. They found ways to care for me even as they farmed the fields, cultivated their vineyards, and raised livestock. The townspeople that I still visit yearly remind me:

> *"While your grandparents worked in the fields, they placed you in the shade and brought along a day's worth of food for you. When you were a little older, you played as your nonno plowed and your nonna sowed potatoes, beans and corn. In the vineyards, you followed your grandpa, while blowing in a whistle your nonno made from vines. You were always the best-dressed child in town, even while taking the cows to pasture. Your grandparents loved you so much!"*

Later, when we returned to the farmhouse, the animals had to be fed and dinner had to be picked, or killed and cooked. Cooking on a wood burning stove or in the black pot inside the fireplace was time-consuming. Even our water had to be pumped from the well in our courtyard. Since the town store only sold dried goods, we had to make other staples from scratch: milk, butter, and cheese, preserves, lard, etc.

For a bi-annual change of bedding, nonna and I brought our marijuana hemp sheets to the river. Nonna knelt by a huge rock slanting toward the water and scrubbed with homemade soap until her knuckles were raw. On the way home, carrying heavy wet sheets in the cart, nonna and I stopped at the brook to catch frogs for a special lunch treat: fried frog legs.

Of course, I had to go to school and nonna accompanied me. During the harsh winters, when the snow reached above our knees, nonna 'plowed' in front of me. After school, she always prepared me a 'merenda': a late afternoon snack of raw eggs beaten with sugar and Marsala wine (now called zabaglione), bread and chocolate, or bread with butter and sugar.

Then I would go to the barn adjacent to our kitchen in order to keep warm, and drink sweet milk squirted into my mouth by nonno as he milked the cows. I loved the feeling of nonno nourishing me this way, but the tuberculosis I contracted from unpasteurized milk eventually made me very ill. I remember feeling awful for years, probably from a high fever. My nonni didn't know I was sick and rationalized my crankiness as a symptom of not having parents.

This could not have been farther from the truth. In my heart, my nonni WERE my parents! I felt no lacking in nurturing and affection—even though I knew I had a mother across the Atlantic.

As to be expected, my mother missed me and wanted me to join the new family she had established in the New World. This was inconceivable to the three of us who had solidified our own family bonds. With time, the endearing letters crossing the Atlantic became an ultimatum. From Detroit, Michigan, my mother wrote:

> *"...now you must make a difficult decision: whether to let my Piera come alone or whether you want to accompany her. I'll tell you again; life is easier here... I know you'll be happier...We can all live in the same house... you'll be able to give Piera the love and support she needs. Otherwise, she might hate me forever for taking her away from you. As it is, bonding will be difficult enough. I beg of you, start selling your livestock and your farm equipment! In*

> *America, we have grocery stores that provide food—already in packages!*
>
> *By the way, the Italian Line told me they have a beautiful ship called the* Andrea Doria. *You can put our entire family trousseau on board and bring it to America..."*

To keep our bonds intact, my grandparents decided to make the ultimate sacrifice: liquidate their farm and accompany me to America.

In the spring of 1956, we bought three tickets on the Italian luxury liner, with my mother's support. The 'unsinkable' *Andrea Doria* represented the finest tradition in art, craftsmanship, architecture, and technology. I know this didn't relieve my nonna's deepest fears; she was simply paranoid when it came to water.

Nevertheless, on July 17, 1956, my grandparents and I boarded the *Andrea Doria.* Pietro and Domenica felt much trepidation, while I felt only excitement. What could be better after all? I would be with my nonni and soon with a new family: a stepfather, a mother, and a one-year-old sister. What I didn't know is that nonna and my mother had never gotten along, and my nonni knew they were about to confront a sensitive personal situation.

The voyage on the *Andrea Doria* was pleasant, except for one day of rough seas. By the eighth day, we felt secure about arriving safely in New York—in spite of the dense fog—along with all the possessions we could carry from our former life in Italy. Nonna was relaxed enough to suggest joining other immigrants for merriment in the Social Hall. Nonno went to sleep in his third class cabin below in preparation for early arrival the next morning.

What happened next was about to obscure my nonni's sacrifices and drown our immigrant dreams. At 11:10 p.m., the Swedish liner *Stockholm* indiscriminately broadsided us at full speed, penetrating one third of our vessel.

> *"We swayed rigidly from an abrupt jolt, accompanied by a thunderous noise. Those who were on the outer deck witnessed startling fireworks created by grinding steel... they watched in horror as the perpetrator tried to withdraw from the hole it had created by slicing through the thick walls of steel that had once protected passengers from the*

*dangers of the ocean. In the Social Hall, these gruesome theatrics were magnified by the crashing of hundreds of bottles that landed on the bar floor, as if thrown there by the devil's rage. Every fiber in our spines reacted to the scraping, screeching, and crunchy noises from an indefinable source."**

Although greatly traumatized, we eventually made it to shore on the French passenger liner, *Ile de France*—with only the clothes on our backs, my nonno's briefcase, and my nonna's purse. Then we flew to Detroit, arriving exhausted, distressed, and scared.

I finally 'met' my mother. Since my nonna had instructed me to hug my mother when I saw her, I did so immediately with all the emotion I could muster.

Then we all crammed into one car which brought us to our new home. Frequent interviews by the media made our daily life a disquieting public affair. There were other challenges too: our house was small, my stepdad didn't speak Italian, one-year-old Marisa cried constantly, and we lacked belongings, friends, and community ties.

The fact that we had been part of the greatest sea rescue in history was never discussed—nor was anything relating to the *Andrea Doria* tragedy. On a day-to-day basis, life was about surviving a difficult family situation. My nonna felt like she was useless baggage living in small quarters; disputes became the norm; acts of jealousy over me ensued between my mother and grandmother; the woman who had curled my hair and dressed me like a princess just to go to pasture no longer had a say over my life. Nonno felt unworthy as an unemployed farmer.

Fortunately, both my grandparents got jobs: nonna as a seamstress, and nonno worked in a lumber yard. Nonna learned English fairly well, unlike nonno, who spoke only Italian with coworkers. He was treated badly by his Italian boss. Feeling unappreciated, he relinquished his only source of income—which luckily spared him a daily 10-mile walk to and from work.

The Promised Land promised only disappointment for my grandparents. Although they eventually moved into a home just down the street from us, the family unit moved toward disintegration: my grandparents went through a bitter divorce, and soon after so did my parents.

~~~~~~

Reflecting upon our tragic voyage, a challenging new life, and difficult family circumstances still evokes pain. But mostly because I was the source for uprooting two loving people in their mid-50s who gave up their past--only to lose all that remained on the Atlantic crossing!

To keep me grounded, I focus on the gratitude I feel for my grandparents' love, upbringing, and sacrifice. I was the most fortunate grandchild in the world. Often, I wonder if I could ever be so grand as to give selfless love, leave my country and community, and start a new life in a strange land for a grandchild. Honestly, I don't know; fortunately, I will never have to know. All that I'm sure of is that Pietro and Domenica Burzio, my nonni, made the ultimate sacrifice for me.

*Excerpt from *Alive on the Andrea Doria! The Greatest Sea Rescue in History*, by Pierette Domenica Simpson, New York, with Morgan James publishing, 2008.

Pierette
Pierette@PieretteSimpson.com
248-349-8557
www.PieretteSimpson.com
www.AndreaDoriabook.com
www.PieretteSimpson.com/blog
New historic audio book

Guest Author Bio: Pierette Domenica Simpson was born in northern Italy, near Torino, and immigrated to the United States as a young girl. Fluent in French, Italian and Spanish, she dedicated her professional career to teaching foreign languages. Upon retiring, Ms. Simpson began her authorial journey, publishing an award-winning book, *Alive on the Andrea Doria! The Greatest Rescue in History*, in print and audio CD. Currently she enjoys speaking about her fateful voyage to America.
~~~~~~

Take a Break

Well, some of those last few stories were a bit heavy and I thought we might use a break. Here are three short stories I wrote in the form of poetic verse, followed by two even shorter story forms.

About Pee

By Steven R Roberts

Every family has a tale about pee
Here's one that happened to me
If you can top this with tales of your own
Send them along to, www.peeinmyear.com

Dads don't take pit stops for the family
Despite desperate requests aplenty
If I don't have to go and we got gas
Wait a couple more miles, the need will pass.

On a freeway one of our boys started to complain
Mom held a Coke bottle to relieve the pain
Standing on the transmission hump in the back seat
Wee Willy into the bottle, speedy, nice and neat.

Dad hit a bump going around a curve
Out came Willy as the car did a swerve
Stream diverted the kids all cheer
"How am I supposed to drive, he's peeing in my ear."

The moral of the story is simply this
Not everyone can wait as long as Dad to piss
But as Dad gets older, the kids drive of late
Dad cries from the back seat, "Hey I can't wait."

An Old Man, An Old Dog

By Steven R Roberts

Old men and old dogs think the same
Of hopes and dreams that never came
They walk the streets, two ends of the lead
Shufflin', Sniffin' spent leaves, half speed.

Roaming hours on paths not there
No need to hurry back, no one to care
Show dog and show man sifting life's sand
Wet eyes meet, old dog and old man.

Rabbits need not fear the chase
Fate delayed not denied, the fall from grace
Breathe nature's juices damp and sweet
Old friends they soon will meet.

Bent in the smoky night chatting away
Bout a long ago busier day
They fought the good fight, right at the time
The last to go will drag the other's end behind.

Lucky's Mob

By Steven R Roberts

I was Lucky Luciano playin' the Piano
Bugsy and Lansky played percussion
New York boys sang soprano
Boo and Waxey the Russian

We had booze, muscle, and book
Runnin', sightless pigs, murder for hire
Dancin' the Feds and cops on the hook
Girls of the night on fire

Detroit streets painted red with Purple
Brothers Bernstein, the meanest ever seen
Izzi, and Hymie, riddlin' bodies that gurgle
The Gorilla givin' protection for green

The Little Jewish Navy runnin' booze 'cross the river
Cops and Coast Guard pinned down on the shore
Workin' for Capone we had better deliver
Zerilli and Frankie makin' machine gun lore

Massacres, Valentines, Milaflores, Collingwood
Egan's Rats makin' mobsters drop
Revenge and greed doin' more than cops ever could
Self-wackin' contracts, impossible to stop

I called a national meet to stop the fightin'
Jersey scene, Capone representin' the hood
Men of murder, tense, some were packin'
Egos and power brought no truce, no good

Booze came back, the law shut us down
Survivors sang or took a chair, brains popped
Savage killers cried a river, what a sound
Even Lucky, wasn't, when the music stopped

Very Short Poems

Moving to an even shorter form of storytelling, this page tells stories in one stanza. These are truncated poems from my 2004 book ***Rhythm and Rhyme Lifetime, Hometown Poetry and Song.*** These life-changing, one-verse poems are in the mode of the works of the poet Ogden Nash.

Ode to a Cat

If you get a cat beware
He'll change your heart, steal your chair
This furry mop with an attitude
Will put you in permanent cat servitude

Digging Dentist

They call him Dr. Tooth
And cavities he'll pursuth
He'll think you're a bit uncouth
If he digs out an old piece of Baby Ruth

What Are Brothers For

Girls have girlfriends. Boys have brothers.
They're a team, a common theme, like no other
Some save their brothers' lives, mine saved mine
It happens, it happens all the time

You Interrupted Me

You interrupted me on my way to nowhere
You found me when I didn't care
Going for broke and I was almost there
Then you gave me a love to share

Mom

Losing your mom takes a piece of your heart
A part of who you are and where you're from
Gone is something you held dear from the start
Lost forever the phrase: "Hey, look at me Mom."

Six-Word Stories

And shorter yet is the six-word story. Hemingway combined poetry and drama and invented a short story form known as the six-word story. Examples include:

- For sale: Baby shoes, Never worn – Ernest Hemingway
- Longed for him, got him. Shit – Margaret Atwood
- Revenge is living well, without you – Joyce Carol Oates
- Woman, without her man, is nothing - Anon
- Woman: without her, man is nothing - Anon

Here are a select few from members of a writers' group I belong to in Florida

- Married young, knew nothing; got lucky
- Alimony: buying hay for dead horses
- Great story, editor rejected, total idiot
- Sorry, I am so unworthy, dear
- Dozing night, ran red light, boom

I'm sure you can think of more ways to tell a very short story in six words. But now, back to our short stories.

Two Phone Calls

By Steven R. Roberts

Eleven people gathered in Mom's living room. No grandkids. No great-grandkids.

There were to be no rings. Mom said the couple's hands were too swollen. There would be no walk down the aisle. The couple wasn't that good at walking, she said. They would sit for the ceremony. My sister and Garrold's son would stand next to the brown folding chairs where the wedding couple would be seated.

Garrold could hear about half of what was going down. He smiled out of respect for the moment. Mom, who had smiled at most everything in her long life, smiled and looked at the preacher. She was pleased to have solved a problem.

"I know it's really up to me," Mom had said in a phone call five years earlier, "but I'd feel better if you approved. It's just a fish dinner at the Elks."

Dad, at 84, had been gone six months and Mom had called from Ohio to ask for my approval before she accepted a dinner date with Garrold, an old friend of the family. I had lived my life looking for my parents' approval, starting with the days of "Look Mom, No Hands" just before I crashed my bike into the neighbor's porch. Mom's phone call for my approval was an interesting twist of events but distance and time had not changed my need to please her.

"Sure, Mom," I said. I found out later that some other family members had objected to the "date" as inappropriate, apparently wanting Dad in the grave another month or two.

"You know, there's no time to wait for the right time," Mom said.

Garrold was a widower the family had known for five decades. From that day on, Garrold and mom were together each Friday at the Elks fish dinner as well as family holidays and other special gatherings. They also played gin rummy three or four nights a week. They were good company for each other.

Nearly five years after the first call, I received another call from Mom.

"Honey, Garrold and I would like to get married," Mom said. "I was wondering if you would have any problem with that."

I paused. "Sure, Mom, if that's what you want," I said finally, trying to hold off on questions I wanted to ask but didn't want to spoil the moment. Why now? Why marriage? Couldn't they just move in together? (Oops, wrong generation.) What if Mom, 88 or Garrold, nearly 93, got sick and put into a long-term care facility? Would the surviving spouse lose all of his or her meager assets? Could one of them become homeless and move in with us? Would the newlyweds agree to raise any kids Catholic? There was a lot to think about.

"Honey, neither one of us wants to drive home after dark. We play gin most evenings and it's particularly bad in the winter with the snow," Mom responded to my silence. I tried not to think of either one of them driving even on a warm dry day in the noon-day sun. However, Mom's answer cleared up a couple of my questions about her plans. It made sense. I knew of another couple who had gotten married for the Blue Cross coverage.

"Reverend Fenway has agreed to perform the ceremony," Mom said, and his fee will be a dozen Pro VI Titleist golf balls. He has also promised to conveniently neglect to register the marriage certificate with the county clerk's office." That answered one of my other questions.

On the day, it was very still in Mom's house. The normal din of noise and commotion of the hoard of grandchildren and great-grandchildren was being kept at a house down the block until the ceremony was over. Instead, the eleven of us sat quietly in her living room. Mom hadn't wanted any music, no Pachelbel's Cannon for her, nothing.

Reverend Fenway walked in quietly, centered himself against the bay window at the back of the room and faced the 11 witnesses. Eventually, the wedding couple emerged from the kitchen with matching walkers. Mom, smiling in her new pink dress, was stunning. She stood as tall as her 88 years would allow, even if only for a moment. Garrold, wearing a beige sports jacket and chocolate brown slacks, held Mom's wrist with one hand and leaned on his walker as they carefully crossed the 15 feet from the kitchen to the folding chairs.

With the help of my sister and Garrold's son the couple got themselves centered over their respective chairs and simultaneously let loose of their walkers. Garrold tried to hold Mom's hand in flight but he missed. The small group of witnesses sat up straight, as Mom would have wanted, and remained quiet.

"Friends, we are gathered here today to…," Reverend Fenway said, calling the meeting to order.

"Mickie, do you take Garrold to be…"

"I do."

"Garrold, do you take Mickie to be…" Reverend Fenway paused.

"Garrold, do you take Mickie to be…" he said much louder.

"Ah, I do."

Meanwhile, the privileged eleven stifled a laugh and a tear or two, comforted with the knowledge that there would be two less lonely people in the world and one less driving that night after dark.

The eleven of us gave the bride and groom a reserved standing ovation.

"God bless you and Garrold, Mom," I prayed.

Author's note: The married couple had many happy months together. Garrold passed away a year after the ceremony and Mom left us in May a year later in 2009. Mom said it was a perfect match. She finally learned how to beat Garrold at gin and he never complained about her playing the radio too loud.

At her funeral, I was reminded of the power of moms in shaping our lives. Like most Moms, she had worried about me and my three siblings as if we were twelve years old all of our lives. With her last breath, Mom aged me from a pre-teen to the oldest survivor in the family.

Author: The Patriarch

Requiem for a Mentor Thanksgiving 1986

By Steven R. Roberts

"Come on in," said Duke Moore, my Vice President. "Let's get started I'd like to get out of here at a decent time tonight."

Walking into his office, I said, "I've only got seven or eight items tonight so it shouldn't take more than 25 minutes."

"Alright, let's cover them here at my desk," he said, waving me away from the conference table.

"We've got a couple of issues with the way Europe is handling the Company's quality standards," I began. "Then there's the Brazil personnel issue you already know about, the Worldwide Supply Managers meeting proposed for May, and we need to respond to the Auditor's report that's proposed to go to the Board next month. The rest are for info only so they can wait."

I had been the Director of Purchasing Policy and Planning (The VP's Chief of Staff) for Duke Moore for almost two years and it was customary for me to brief the boss each day on issues that needed his attention. These sessions were usually at the end of a long day so they needed to be to the point, and with proposed solutions rather than questions. I had worked directly and indirectly for Duke for 15 of my 25 years at Ford. Duke was known as a hard charger, smart as a whip and suffering no fools. He liked to get right to the point and insisted on getting the job done no matter what it took. Over our long careers with the Company, we had gotten used to long days, lots of travel and tight schedules.

It was the day before Thanksgiving and I had the 5:45 pm time slot, the last of the day for both of us. Duke's office was on the 12th floor of the Ford World Headquarters. It was large enough for a half court game of basketball; dark paneled with a large mahogany conference table and desk, along with a couch and assorted tables and chairs. An end table just inside the door held 17 pictures of his family at various stages of development.

"First, we need to give our final approval to the five new personnel appointments in Brazil and Argentina," I said. "These are the candidates we discussed last week and I've covered them with the office heads down there."

Representing Duke's office, I worked with the General Managers of our offices in other countries on replacement scenarios for filling openings. Duke had to sign off of personnel appointments at our facilities around the globe.

"Is Mike ready to take on straightening out this mess in Brazil?" Duke asked looking at the list of personnel moves. "Is his family all set?"

"Mike says Sandy and the two boys are ready for the adventure, even though the older boy has to leave his tenth grade hockey career behind for a while," I reported. "Mike's a straight shooter and he ought to be able to survive and make a difference in the ethics mess they've gotten into."

The strictest business ethics were important to Duke. His success had been partly due to his ability to take the high road on business ethics, even gaining a reputation as a young supervisor by refusing to accept even a ballpoint pen from a supplier. The other reasons he had risen to the rank of Vice President of the second largest company in the world were that he was very intelligent, smooth and tough depending on what was best for the company. In one famous incident, after negotiating a very favorable deal with a supplier, he was promoted from the manager level to Executive Director, jumping over the head of his own boss. The following day his former boss was reporting to Duke.

"OK," Duke said, "write up Mike's announcement letters for Brazil and the others."

"The personnel announcement letters are ready for your signature," I said. "They're effective the first of next month." I slid the letters across the desk for Duke to sign.

On that late Wednesday night, Thanksgiving eve 1986, I reviewed and obtained Duke's approval or instructions on three other items on my agenda.

Finally I said, "The last thing is that I have reviewed the Auditor's report on supplier audits for the year to date and unfortunately the trend of higher charge-backs to suppliers for fraudulent billings continues." I was just confirming what Duke already knew from our preliminary discussion earlier in the week.

"Damn these guys," Duke said. "Do they really think putting on more auditors will get them more charge-backs? Of course it will. The suppliers know these guys need to find something to justify their existence so they just start putting a little extra in their tool bills to keep them happy. I've got to talk to Redding (the Company's President, Augustus Redding) about the ethics of this whole process and..."

Suddenly Duke stopped talking and abruptly stood up at his desk. "Man, do I have a headache." He said holding on to the desk to steady himself. "It's like a knife."

I hadn't really observed this kind of reaction from Duke over the years, but I knew he hated this auditing topic. Assuming he wanted to get this meeting over with, I said, "Duke, why don't I write up a proposed change in the process which would make it clear to the suppliers and the auditors which items are acceptable as tooling and which aren't."

"Damn, this is the worst headache I've ever had." Duke said pacing behind his desk, periodically holding onto it for support. "My God, I can't get any relief, it won't stop, it's like a knife behind by left ear," he said. Finally he sat down hard, just sat there holding his head with both hands, elbows on his desk.

"Duke, I'm going to call Medical and see if anybody's still there," I said, proceeding out of the office to place the call from his secretary's phone. It was 6:20 pm on a holiday weekend and I was worried about getting anybody in Medical.

"Medical," said a voice on the other end of the line. It was Liz, the World Headquarters head nurse.

Recognizing her voice, I introduced myself. "Liz, I'm up on 12 in a meeting with Mr. Moore. I think he's having a stroke or an aneurysm of some kind. Is the doctor there?"

"No, he's gone for the day and I was just going out the door, so it's lucky you called when you did. I'll be right up."

I went back into Duke's office and told him the nurse was on the way. I'm not sure he heard me. By now he had his head down leaning on his hands, which were lying on his desk.

"Duke, are you still with me?" I asked. "I'm going to call an ambulance and Mrs. Moore while we're waiting for Liz." I called the hospital and was calling Mrs. Moore as Liz arrived.

"His wife is going to meet us at Oakwood Hospital. She's going to pick up their daughter to come with her," I told Liz. I explained the sequence of events leading up to my call to the Medical office.

"Hurry, this is the most piercing pain I've ever felt in my life," came a pained response from Duke. He tried to stand and fell back into his chair.

Liz tried to talk to Duke to determine his state of consciousness but she couldn't get a response. She helped steady Duke while I placed his arm over my shoulder. I walked him out into the hall leading to the freight elevator where Liz had said the Oakwood ambulance team would come up.

Duke was still alert enough to support half of his weight but I could feel him go limp as we moved slowly down the hall. Half way to the elevator Dave McKinnon, the Company's head of Finance, heard the commotion and came out of his office to help. The elevator door opened just as we got there and the ambulance attendants put Duke on the gurney.

"I'll go back to my office and call Dr. Assenmacher, (the Company's head of medical affairs). I'll see you at the hospital," Liz said, hurrying back down the hall.

Oakwood Hospital is centrally-located among several of the company's buildings and plants. The staff was quick to realize the gravity of the situation for the patient wheeled into the emergency room that night. He was taken into Emergency immediately and within 20 minutes Duke was being attended by the hospital's head of neurology. The chief surgeon for brain surgery was on his way to the hospital.

One of the nurses brought out a small paper sack with Duke's watch, keys and billfold and gave it to Liz to give to Mrs. Moore when she arrived. Liz brought the sack to me. "Steve, I'm terrible at this kind of thing. I'll start crying and won't get through it. You've got to talk to Mrs. Moore and give her his personal items."

I agreed, although I couldn't help but believe that Liz must have had more experience with this kind of thing than I did, which was none.

Just then Mrs. Moore and her daughter came through the Emergency door and we shook hands and sat together. I explained what had happened from the time Duke alerted me to the pain he was suffering. I wasn't sure if I should shake her hand so I didn't. I just stood there holding the paper sack with her husband's personal belongings, trying to think when the right time would be to give it to her. The following moments of silence were broken by the hospital's head of neurology, who came out to discuss Duke's medical situation.

"Mr. Moore has had a massive brain aneurysm and there is considerable pressure on the cranial cavity," he reported. "We think surgery will be required, either now or in the morning to relieve the pressure."

"Is there permanent brain damage?" asked Mrs. Moore tentatively.

"At this point we don't know. We're still reviewing the Cat scans and we're going to do an MRI in a few minutes to help us assess his condition." With that the doctor was gone, back through the swinging doors of the Emergency room.

I turned to Mrs. Moore and gave her the sack. She opened the paper sack and stared, along with her daughter, at the items her husband had in his pants pockets when he was admitted to the hospital.

After a while Dr. Assenmacher, a tall man with wavy gray hair and thick glasses, came out of the back rooms of the Emergency area and sat down with us. He leaned close to Mrs. Moore, explaining his understanding of Duke's condition.

"The MRI has confirmed that Duke has a massive brain aneurysm," the doctor said. "To have the best chance of saving his brain function, I recommend we operate immediately."

"I see," Mrs. Moore whispered, her hands trembling in her lap. "Do you have a recommendation on the surgeon?"

"Definitely, the best two brain surgeons are Dr. Keller and Dr. Chan. Both operate out of Henry Ford Hospital downtown," Assenmacher said. "We need to get Duke there immediately and I've got their helicopter on the way. I assumed you would agree."

"Yes, of course," Mrs. Moore said. "Can I see Duke for a minute? Can I ride in the helicopter with him?"

"Sure," Assenmacher said, "let me set it up and then I'll see you up at Henry Ford. They're getting him ready now and we'll need to leave within 10 minutes. It'll take another 10 to fly to the hospital."

"Liz, you can go home and I'll drive to Henry Ford to make sure things are okay there," I said. "Thanks for your help."

"You've got my home number if for some reason you need me up there," Liz reminded me as she got ready to go. She seemed anxious to leave.

I left Oakwood by car just as the helicopter was lifting off for Henry Ford. During my 30-minute ride, I thought of the years Duke Moore and I had worked together and how important he had been in my work-life and in my life in general. We had been through periods of nearly round-the-clock work sessions, trying to resolve materials issues which were threatening to shut down manufacturing plants and send 4,000 to 5,000 workers home for a day or two. At times there were late-night flights to suppliers' plants to resolve cost and production problems that threatened to shut down the majority of the Company's plants. Duke, along with Chet, his next in command, had been key players in sending me and my family to work in Europe for three years on the first "worldwide common design car" – the Escort. And he was the one who brought me back to be his chief of staff.

He was tough, he was precise, and he played the big shot when it was appropriate, receiving and giving out awards in various countries and to suppliers at plant openings and quality award ceremonies. He was also self-effacing when a dose of humor suited the situation.

Once, when I was arranging a visit to Venezuela, the General Manager was resisting me on some of the arrangements - hotels, dinner meeting arrangements, flights, etc. Duke heard about my problems and told me to tell the country's manager he could make the trip arrangements but he wanted the car that met us at the airport to drive out on the tarmac close to the end of the steps from the plane. "Let him know I expect a red carpet from the plane steps to the limousine," Duke said. "I don't want my Gucci shoes to ever come in contact with cement. Tell him that is the kind of attention to detail I want during our whole visit."

By the time I got to Henry Ford Hospital, the helicopter had arrived and the emergency team had taken Duke into the intensive care unit for evaluation.

I sat and talked with Mrs. Moore, their daughter, and Dr. Assenmacher for an hour on that Thanksgiving Eve. We knew tomorrow and probably the rest of the Thanksgivings of our lives were never going to be quite the same, but we weren't sure how the night and the next day were going to play out.

When the team of doctors finished their examination and evaluation they came to see us in the waiting room. "There's no question that we need to operate immediately," reported Dr. Keller. "The pressure on Mr. Moore's brain is severe due to the blood clot, and the chance of severe brain damage occurring as we speak is almost certain."

Mrs. Moore and Dr. Assenmacher exchanged nodding glances and agreed. "Please proceed immediately," the Company doctor said.

It was 11:15 pm and the operation was to take more than an hour, followed by post-op recovery during the rest of the night. Mrs. Moore and her daughter were going to stay for a while. I said my good-byes and agreed to see them in the waiting room the next morning. As I left, I apologized for having to make such a terrible call to her earlier in the day.

Mrs. Moore was crying gently. "I had been waiting for a call like yours for the last 20 years," she said. "I just thought he probably wouldn't walk out of there (the Company) alive."

It was midnight when I pulled into the driveway at home. Our four kids were sleeping but Jane and our black lab, Bella, were waiting up for me. Jane and I promised each other that we'd give an extra prayer for the Moore family at the next day's family Thanksgiving dinner. We knew there would be years of hard work ahead to survive and thrive in the Company, but we agreed to make sure both of us got out alive.

"Good morning" was the only thing I could think of to say to the Moore family gathered in the waiting room that Thanksgiving morning. "How's Duke doing?"

"He made it through two operations to relieve pressure on his brain last night," Mrs. Moore said. "The pressure is gone and he has been resting comfortably. We're just waiting on the doctors' latest assessments."

"Well, that's good, very good," I said. "We all knew he was in great pain last night at Oakwood. Have they said anything about the long-term situation?" I asked, knowing the question was on everyone's mind.

"What we know is the news is not too good." I could tell Mrs. Moore knew more than she was saying. "The doctors say Duke has permanent brain damage and probably won't make it," Mrs. Moore said, as she sat on a couch in the middle of a family gathering in the otherwise deserted waiting room.

The daughter summed it up. "Daddy always told us to use our brains. He was always about being smart and the power of intelligence," she said. "Now they say Daddy's brain is gone." There were tears in her eyes and in her voice. "It's hard to believe the Daddy we knew is gone. He was always there and will never be there again."

The life support systems were turned off later that day and Duke Moore, my boss and friend for over 25 years, was dead by mid-afternoon, Thanksgiving Day.

Just about that time, Jane and I and our four children were sitting down to Thanksgiving dinner. We gave a hug to each other and a special prayer for the Moore family and for our own. I had three days to think about my vision, my approach to balancing the Company's needs with my family's. There were three days before Monday morning.

Author's Note: Unfortunately this is a true story about the time surrounding Thanksgiving 1986 when I lost my mentor and friend. Only the names have been changed.

Charlie Boggs

By Steven R. Roberts

He couldn't help himself. Charlie recognized the sound of a racing motor vehicle coming down the hall before any of his 10th grade classmates. He was the first to bolt toward the door to have a look. Right behind him, pushing for a peek, came, Bones Barnes and T.J. Epley, along with the rest of the class. Jammed five deep into the doorway, they stretched out into the hall as the breeze of the speeding jeep, the smell of exhaust and rumble of a cracked muffler went rumbling by the first time.

"Sit down!" Penny Ellison said in the gritty military voice she used when class reaction was slow. The math teacher had been in the small storage room when the class leaped from their seats. Jim Karrick, who everybody knew as "Bo", and Brian "Spitter" Daly were driving a jeep down the Perrysburg High hallway the final week of their senior year. Bo and Spitter, a name he got playing third base for the school's baseball team, had disassembled the middle post from the double doors coming out of the Industrial Arts wing. Bo proceeded to drive his green army jeep, squealing tires and blasting WOWO rock and roll, down the school's front hallway. The second hour classes were finishing their session when the happening in the hall caused the students to slam their books closed and hurry for a look at the delicious spectacle. Behind them in each room was an indignant teacher commanding the students back into their seats.

Bo made a turn toward the auditorium doors at the far end of the second hallway. That's when the two boys discovered there wasn't enough room to turn the vehicle around. Bo jammed the transmission into reverse and the rear tires squealed around the corner heading back past Charlie's classroom. Reaching the lobby, Bo was in the process of trying to turn around by pushing the stuffed chairs and couches aside with the jeep's rear bumper when Cappy Sinclair stepped out of his office. Mr. Sinclair, the tall disheveled assistant principal, peered through his smudged horned-rimmed glasses and blocked the path of the vehicle. He widened his stance and held his hand out for the keys. The jeep's tires slid to a stop on the waxed floor inches from the assistant principal's shins.

Bo and Spitter were marched into the principal's office and not seen again the rest of the day. The jeep was gone by third hour and the two adventurers' diplomas were held for three weeks after graduation. That was until Bo's dad, a local lawyer, drove out to Roachton Road and paid a visit to the principal's office.

Back in room 118, Charlie Boggs and the rest of Miss Ellison's math class received detention for two nights. Charlie's father would restrict him to the house for a week when word got around about the incident.

"How do they think of stupid tricks like that?" Epley asked, sitting with Charlie in detention. "I know they're going to catch holy hell, but what kind of a high must you get for blasting the rules to pieces like that?"

"Stupid is the right word for it," Charlie said.

"Charlie, lighten up a bit, will ya?" Epley whispered. "Nobody got hurt and besides, don't you see, that's the kind of innovative thinking they're trying to pound into our heads around here. What must it be like? We are going to remember the backward speeding jeep in the halls of school for the rest of our lives." Epley leaned back in his chair and clasped his hands behind his unruly mop of black wavy hair. "Wouldn't it be worth a little crap to set a standard for pranks like that?"

"Innovative maybe, but that was stupidity," Charlie said. "They'll need some new thinking to get out of the trouble coming their way. I'm sure my dad will say they should get some jail time."

"Questions about your homework, gentlemen?" Mr. Rusler, the detention room monitor, asked, approaching from the rear of the room.

That was the end of the longest conversation Charlie had ever had with Epley during their three years of high school. It was nearly the longest conversation Charlie had with anyone during high school with the exception of his nerdy friend, Harley Botts, who he sat next to in every class.

Years later Charlie realized Epley was right. Indeed, Charlie did remember the incident even when he was 42. For all of those years in between Charlie wondered what it would have been like to venture off the main road, to take the path less traveled. He had always been an avid observer of the adventurers around him, and yet he had traveled exclusively between the curbs. Now look where it had gotten him. Charlie thought of his life as a long flat spot somehow tilted down so the sweet juices drained off into the dirt. He was sliding gently toward hell without ever deserving to go in that direction. That was until yesterday. Now he was speeding south on I-69, trying to avoid a police dragnet committed to catching him and his accomplice.

Speed hadn't been part of Charlie's early life in his birth place, Perrysburg, Ohio. With a population around 14,000, Perrysburg was a crisp and clean, historic town on the banks of the Maumee River. Charlie had followed the family guidelines laid down by his parents as well as the small town society. Three interdependent forces shaped his early years in a small town – parents, schools and community. If you received a paddling from a teacher at school (which Charlie never did), you knew you'd get a paddling for getting a paddling when you got home. In high school, Charlie walked away from or talked his way out of fights and avoided confrontation, and even the perception of impropriety, whenever he could.

Russell Boggs, Charlie's dad, ran a small diner near the corner of Louisianna and Second, a few blocks from the river. Russell had purchased Rinock's Café on land contract from old Fred Rinock and his brother, Bubbles, when they took Fred off to the home and Bubbles retired to somewhere in New Mexico. Russell was a slight man with thinning sandy hair and a matching droopy mustache. He had started in the café as a dishwasher when he dropped out of school at 15 and later became the short-order cook. The café was popular with local farmers and fishermen. It was not popular with school kids, but Charlie found the stories from the customers quite intriguing.

"A wave kicked my feet out from under me," said old Captain Wheelbarger, one of the rusty regulars at Rinock's. The captain loved telling tales of the sea more than he loved fishing. "A three-foot catfish jumped on deck and was sliding toward me when..."

"I know, I know, don't tell me," Russell said. "The giant fish attacked sticking his whiskers into your belly. You pulled him out and heaved him against the hull, knocking him out. When the fish woke up he was sizzling in a frying pan." Russell and the other regulars laughed and so did Wheelbarger. Over the years, the captain's tales of life on Lake Erie got better with each telling.

"Charlie, don't you pay no mind to the captain," Charlie's mother, Allison said. Working every day as the café's cashier, she'd heard the story many times.

Charlie loved working in the café and listening to the stories. He would have quit school and worked in the café full time but Russell insisted he finish what he'd started. While they worked, Mr. Boggs advised his son on several other principles for living. "Start at the bottom and learn," was another bit of advice along with the often repeated, "A penis has no conscience. Don't trust it to do the right thing."

By high school Charlie had grown into a six-foot-one-inch string bean. His father insisted he take up a sport, so Charlie chose NASCAR and collected driver cards. On the weekends he watched the races on a small snowy TV hooked up in the restaurant kitchen.

After graduating with average grades, Charlie and his dad drove to Bowling Green and enrolled him in the university. He commuted from home his first two years and then moved to a house next to campus with his classmate, Luke Butterfield. Luke was a barrel-chested, floppy-haired journalism student from Lima, Ohio. While Luke had a mild disposition to match Charlie's, his wide blue eyes made him appear surprised, maybe even amazed, no matter what was said to him.

"I got a job working on the school newspaper," Luke said the second evening after school. "It's a volunteer job but good for the resume. How about you?"

"I'm working three afternoons a week helping as an accounting clerk for the Holiday Inn. That should be enough to keep both of us out of trouble," Charlie said, repeating a refrain he'd heard his father say many times.

Charlie and Luke were aware of campus parties, sports rallies, social life, binge drinking and the inevitable college pranks going on but they stayed uninvolved and out of trouble. Charlie's dad drilled his son on the reasons he was at school and the reasons had nothing to do with an active social life. It was not surprising that the guys didn't go out much. That changed, however, one night after a discussion over a vanilla shake at the McDonald's across from the football stadium. The Bowling Green-Central Michigan game was in progress and the noise from the local crowd meant BG was winning.

"You going to get married?" Luke asked, as three girls in full bloom came in and walked by their table.

"Sure, it's the thing to do, I guess," Charlie said. "I'd like to move back to Perrysburg and get a job after graduation, but I think I'll need to put some distance between me and the family. Why are you asking? Did you think of having one of those girls' babies?"

"No, I was just wondering what you are going to do, that's all," Luke said. "I was figuring that it takes a while to find somebody and school is probably the best chance we will ever have."

"You mean we had better get started?" Charlie asked. "You're probably right."

The two roommates challenged each other to get into the hunt for a wife. Of course, neither had ever had a girlfriend before so it was quite an uphill climb, with a few falls and tumbles down the dating mountainside.

Luke was afraid of getting rejected by girls so he usually asked for a date through a third party.

"Would you mind asking Ducky if she would mind if I walked her home after work," Luke has said to Marilyn another volunteer working on the school newspaper.

"I thought I was going to have to ask you," Ducky said, a few minutes later giving Luke a gentle punch to the shoulder. Ducky was a buxom blonde from Van Wert, Ohio, and she liked to laugh.

"Good," a wide eyed Luke said, unable to think of anything else to say. "Yea, that's good."

They walked into a cold November wind toward her dorm. Luke didn't know what to do with his hands. They were quivering gently by his sides.

With Ducky supplying more than her share of the conversation and laughs, they seemed to be getting along well. That was true up until the point she turned to face him, pushing her chest into his.

"Guess a girl's got to steal a kiss to get one from you, Luke. Don't seem to be any comin' my way otherwise," Ducky said, wrapping her hand behind his neck and pulling Luke into her.

Luke's first kiss caused his hands to freeze and his eyes to go wet. He was choking and out of breath when he suddenly felt embarrassed and broke away. He looked down at his stiff hands and then back to Ducky.

"Don't look so surprised, Lukie. And don't tell me you didn't like that," Ducky laughed, pressing forward. "I've been watching that kisser of yours for all these weeks, wanting for a little taste." She reached over and put her hand around his mouth, pulling his lips into an exaggerated pucker, then she kissed him again. Luke squeezed his eyes closed and then suddenly opened them wide as her tongue slipped slowly between his teeth and painted the inside of his mouth.

Luke bounced back a step. His ears were ringing. He felt dizzy and turned to run, falling over another couple wrestling on the grass in the dark. Luke scrambled to his feet and ran all the way to his room. The next day he called the school paper to resign. He never talked to Ducky again and luckily, he said, she didn't call him. Luke was embarrassed and mystified by the incident and swore Charlie to a lifetime of secrecy.

Charlie met Minnie at the beginning of a new semester in his bowling class, when they both reached for the same ball on the rack. Minnie had grown up in Findlay, about 30 miles south of campus. Her father worked for the sugar company and her mom was a teacher. At 5'8", Minnie had blue eyes, a warm smile and long, wavy brown hair. She had a little dimple to the right of her mouth when she smiled. Charlie thought she was the most beautiful girl he'd ever seen.

During the course of a long courtship, they managed to graduate; Charlie with an accounting degree and Minnie with a degree in education. After some false starts, they both found jobs in nearby Fort Wayne, Indiana. The wedding was held at St. Michael's in Findlay and the reception was at the Findlay Country Club along the Blanchard River.

By 4:30 in the afternoon Charlie's mom, Allison, had downed four glasses of pink champagne and threw up in the river. She knelt and scooped a handful of water from the flowing river to wash her face. It was a funny spectacle, but Russell refused to speak to his wife for the rest of the day, as well as during the drive back to Perrysburg.

The new couple moved into a middle-class neighborhood of wood-sided homes on Leesmore Lane in west Fort Wayne and set up the base for their two careers. Living in this house, they worked without incident or children, making mediocrity fashionable, for the next two decades. Vacations each year consisted of visiting their families in Perrysburg and Findlay. Sometimes Charlie would work in the café during visits to help his father and see old friends.

Then, on a rainy day in May 2005, Charlie's company was sold to the Swiss and the Fort Wayne operation was closed, sending the employees home without jobs.

When Charlie told Minnie the news, he was surprised she wasn't more sympathetic. He expected understanding, compassion and empathy. He sensed disappointment, anger and possibly, confirmation. His between-the-curbs approach had failed at last and Minnie seemed to be telling Charlie, "I told you so."

"You are your Dad, Charlie. Did you ever think that might be the problem?" she asked in a tone that struck deep into Charlie's heart. "My sweet, lovable Charlie, you are your father's age in a younger man's body, right down to your whitey-tidy briefs. Your new mustache has put the finishing touch on the picture."

"What the hell do you want from me?" Charlie asked. "How do you know what kind of underwear my father wears?"

"I don't know, Charlie," Minnie said, closing her eyes and slowly shaking her head, "but there has got to be more to life than the life we have here in this house. Work only has meaning if it leads to something, and lately I don't think we're going anywhere. Do you ever think of where we are going, Charlie?"

"I'm going to sit on the porch," Charlie sighed, taking a Coke from the fridge and letting the screen door spring have a go at bringing the door firmly closed. He couldn't believe the evening was going as badly as the day. Frankly, he'd never noticed Minnie's unhappiness, her longing for a different life. She was in her 22nd year of teaching third grade and she seemed to enjoy her job. They talked occasionally at dinner about her classes over the years but nothing too specific. What the hell did she mean by saying he had become his father? That hurt.

That Friday Minnie walked out on the porch with a cup of coffee.

"Charlie," she said, "I have some bad news to tell you. I was going to tell you two days ago but that didn't seem fair, just after you got the news on your job. There never seems to be a right time, Charlie," she said, taking a breath.

"Don't worry, hon. I'm 42-years-old, out of work and I was turned down twice for a job today. How much worse can it get?" Charlie said, forcing a smile and looking up at his wife. "Have a seat. How did your day go?"

Minnie sat down in the other porch chair and took a sip of her coffee, holding it in both hands.

"Charlie, I need to say this. I have been seeing someone."

"You mean a doctor? What's wrong, Minnie?"

"No, Charlie, listen to me for once. I've been seeing someone, you know, dating or whatever it's called these days, and it has been going on for some time."

"I see why you need a doctor."

"The truth is, Charlie, we have fallen in love. I want to leave to be with him."

Charlie paused, looking in the top of his Coke bottle, which was half way to his mouth.

Minnie went on to say she had been having an affair with the school's sixth grade teacher. It had been going on for a year, and Minnie expressed regrets that it had happened. She wanted a divorce and she would be moving out the following weekend.

Charlie was too stunned to know how to react. He lifted the bottle and took a sip.

"Charlie, I'm really sorry," Minnie said, reaching over to touch his arm. "I tried to ..." Charlie waved her hand away and looked at the porch floor, shaking his head, not wanting to know more.

"Is there a possibility that you are wrong?" he asked.

"No, I don't think so, Charlie. I'm really sorry," Minnie said. She stood and went back in the house, leaving her half a cup of coffee on the small plastic table beside her chair.

The day Minnie left, Charlie sat on the front porch staring at the cars going by on Leesmore and listening to the trucks rumbling down nearby I-69. In the days to come he would sit there for hours on end.

Two weeks after Minnie left, a mutual friend let Charlie know the sixth grade teacher wasn't the first time Minnie had wavered. Apparently she had advanced from a heated affair a couple of years earlier with a fourth grade teacher.

There was really nowhere to go. A visit to Perrysburg was not in order. Charlie's dad had passed away two years earlier, six months to the day after his Mom died. The café had fallen on hard times as the chain restaurants – beginning when an IHOP and a Burger King – moved into town. Russell had been forced to sell a year before his death to meet his debts.

So, this sorry state of affairs is what it had all added up to after all these years, Charlie thought, looking at the spring rains roughing up the puddles in the gutters on the street. As the days passed, he couldn't help but return to his thoughts of long ago. His mind was flat. His life was flat and going worse from that. Was that the problem? Was this his chance to do it a different way, or a chance to become more stupid than he'd ever been in his life? What would it have felt like to have been in that jeep with Bo and Spitter? What would it feel like if he tried it now?

Slowly mixing self-pity, sorrow and rage, Charlie drove his father's lumbering Grand Marquis across the state line to Lima, Ohio. He checked the local phone book and asked a gas station attendant for directions to Prospect Avenue. He climbed the steps to a little turquoise colored house at 602 and rang the bell. A look around told Charlie this had been a nice neighborhood at one time but now the houses, mostly from the 1940s and 50s, had seen better days. Getting no response at the door, he left a note. Walking back to his car, he could see an ornate house in the next block painted three shades of purple.

The next morning a call to his motel room woke Charlie from a sound sleep.

"Charlie, what the hell are you doing, tracking me down?" Luke said. "I haven't seen you since that fishing trip to Canada. I thought you and Minnie were over in Fort Wayne."

Over burgers and Cokes at the Kewpee they updated each other. Luke was truly surprised at the news about Minnie and the divorce. Up until a year earlier Luke had been driving an 18-wheel rig for Duff Trucking. For seven years, he said, he had been making long hauls into the warehouse districts of Detroit and Philadelphia, the dangerous "drive-on-your-flats" areas, he said.

"You seeing anyone special?" Charlie asked, noting that his friend had developed quite a gut sitting hours on end driving a truck.

"Naw, haven't got the energy for the game, I guess."

"What ever happened to the girl from Cincinnati? The one you were dating a few years back."

"I don't know," Luke said. "It lasted longer than most, but a long-haul truck driver is not the best choice for fulfilling a girl's emotional needs, you know? What have you been doing since the divorce?"

"Sitting around feeling sorry for myself and running out of money," Charlie said, leaning back in his tubular chair. "I guess I forgot to tell you I also lost my job two months ago. Actually, Luke, that's what I drove over to talk to you about."

"You came to borrow money?" Luke asked, laughing.

"No, nothing like that. Look, Luke, I've been getting madder by the day. We have sacrificed, you and me, and worked steady for years and now I see we're not getting anywhere. In fact we're going backwards. So far, we didn't get the girl or the money in this movie and the film is on its final reel. I figure we've got one last chance to break through to the other side, to make some big money, to see how it feels to mean something when we walk into a room, and to get what's coming to us before we check out of this ball of dirt. I read someplace that the British have an obsession with getting safely into their graves without embarrassing themselves. Luke, don't you see, we've always acted like the Brits without realizing it."

"That may be, Charlie, but I'm not sure we can make money just by going crazy. We've got to have a plan."

"I've got a plan," Charlie said. "I just need to know you're with me on this. I need you to want to feel the rush of the maverick, the rebel and maybe the outlaw. I see guys getting instant rewards every day while you and I are getting old in life's mirror. You remember the jeep incident I told you about at my high school with two guys named Bo and Spitter? Whatever happened to them? I'll tell you what, nothing. I saw the same thing at work. There's this redneck guy, Curtis Breese, on the shipping dock who has been sacking in with the redheaded, Rhonda, in Receivables, for a couple of years. His only consequence is, you guessed it, nothing but more sacking in with Rhonda."

"Okay, let's talk about our needs," Charlie continued. "It's fairly simple, Luke, as I see it, we need girls and money."

"Don't look at me," Luke said, looking around to see if any Kewpee patrons were listening in on this conversation. "My record is not too stellar in either of those fields."

"Don't worry; we got seven years of advanced education between us and I've had lots of time to work on a fool-proof plan. The money comes first and then we can attract a better class of girls."

"Better class of girls? Are you kidding?" Luke said. "I'd settle for any class of girls. You got a bank in mind?"

"No, banks are too secure. I'm thinking of places that have high amounts of cash during certain times with mid-level security systems. I'm thinking about bars that attract customers by offering to cash paychecks on Fridays. Lots of people stop at these places for a drink and to cash their checks at the end of the week."

"Charlie, you're talking about robbery," Luke said, an octave higher than usual. He stood and began to pace the floor behind the table. Luke's eyes were as big as 50-cent pieces. "Did you see the pies they have when we came in? I need a piece of that pie. You want a piece?"

"No I'm fine. On second thought, sure."

"You don't even have a gun," Luke said, returning with two pieces of cherry pie alamode.

"Don't worry about that. I've got a gun. If we approach this in an organized manner we won't need to show it. Look, I've got a place picked out. There's a bar in Fort Wayne called the Piston Place and I've gone there two Fridays in a row. I took note of the number of paychecks cashed each night and it's somewhere around 100. Most of the factories around the bar are on a two-week pay period, so I figure the average check is for around $ 2,000. If that's right, the bar would have to bring in around $ 250,000 for the evening. "

"Are you nuts?" Luke asked, looking over his shoulder at a nearby table of ladies who looked like they might be nuns in street clothes. "Those machine jockeys from the factories will tear us apart."

"Not necessarily. They won't be there. The way I figure, the bar gets its shipment about 1:00 pm. That means the money is there at least an hour and a half ahead of the end of the first shift. We could hit the bar and be gone before the factory workers get there."

"What about the safe?" Luke asked.

"I think a little shotgun waved at the bartender might convince him to open the safe before I take real aim."

"You're planning on carrying a shotgun into a bar?"

"I'll take care of dad's shotgun; you just drive his old Grand Marquis."

"Jesus, Charlie, this ain't driving a jeep down the hall at school," Luke said. "Couldn't we find another way to break out of mediocre city? How about if we go over to Senior High and drive my old pickup down the hall?"

At 1:30 in the afternoon the following Friday, Charlie and Luke entered Piston Place in Ft Wayne and sat at the bar. The only other patrons were two people eating a late lunch in the back booth. Charlie was wearing a raincoat despite the mild day outside.

"Afternoon," said the barkeep, "what can I get you boys?"

"Two draft beers, Susie," Charlie said, trying to remember to breathe. He could feel his heart beating in the temples on both sides of his head. Charlie had never been so far out of his element.

"The name's Lisa Lu. What kind of draft? We've got Strohs and Coors but the Coors tap ain't workin' today."

"Guess we'll have two Strohs then."

"Comin' up," Lisa Lu said, leaning down to get two clean mugs.

Luke's wide awake gaze was switching focus between the safe and drifting back to Lisa Lu's jump-inside cleavage. They drank their beers too fast and ordered another round.

"Where you boys from?" the barkeep asked. "What you doing' out in the middle of the day, looking for girls?" It was easy to see why Lisa Lu had been hired to handle the customers in a working man's bar. Her deep blue eyes and dishwater blonde hair tied low on her neck made

Charlie think she was probably the center of attention when she was in school. The quarterbacks were all gone now for Lisa Lu, but Charlie bet there'd be guys coming in to cash their paychecks just to talk dirty with her. Suddenly, Charlie remembered his mission. Regaining his focus, he took a deep breath and headed into uncharted waters.

"Look, we don't want any trouble, lady," Charlie said in a voice of false bravado. He pulled the barrel of his shotgun from under his raincoat, ripping out the pocket of the coat in the process. He frowned deeply and laid the shotgun on the bar.

"Whoa there, Jesse James. Easy with the long barrel," the barkeep said. "That thing might go off and tear a bigger hole in your favorite raincoat."

"I'll take it easy. You just listen up, Sister Susie. We know you received today's shipment of cash about an hour ago and we want you to open the safe and give it to us. A little speed would be appreciated."

"You are out of your God damn mind, old man," she said. "I told you my name ain't Susie and I sure as hell ain't no nun."

"Quiet." This woman was getting on Charlie's nerves. Luke was yelling in Charlie's ear and trying to pull him off the barstool toward the door. "Dammit, just open the safe and we'll be out of here."

"I don't even know the combination," Lisa Lu said, "and if I did, I wouldn't open it for you. The boss will be here in a few minutes and he is the only one with…"

"Stop," Charlie said, in a calming voice. "Lady, you are dealing with men trained in the art of thievery. I was in here two weeks ago and I saw you cashing checks out of that safe. I'm going to count to two and then start firing if you don't open the safe. We are desperate drug addicts, my partner, Rocky and I, and we will do anything to get that money. Just look at his eyes. You can tell he needs a fix, quick."

With that, Charlie raised the barrel of the shotgun and fired a blast over the barkeep's head. The buckshot shattered two rows of booze bottles and the large mirror behind the bar, sending brown liquid running down the wall onto the back shelf and shards of glass in all directions. Luke, his eyes as big as ping-pong balls, hit the floor; the couple finishing their late lunch in the back booth huddled under their table. The barkeep fell face down behind the bar; yelling something about busting Charlie's head and making him clean up the mess.

Charlie's eyes watered and then shut at the surprisingly loud sound the shotgun made indoors, but he blinked and stood his ground.

"Open the safe, lady!" he shouted in the midst of the chaos.

Charlie crawled up on the bar and looked down at the barmaid who was frozen, face down to the floor. She was cursing in a low pre-attack whisper.

"Lady, I said open the safe. If you don't I'll have to shoot you." Charlie paused for a couple of seconds and then, for lack of a better target, he lowered his gun and fired a second shot, causing more glass and debris to hit the walls and ricochet around the bar. Luke and the woman under the table both screamed, thinking Charlie had killed Lisa Lu.

"Hey, what the hell are you doing, Jesse James?" shouted the owner coming through the back entrance of the bar. Charlie was quick to reload his father's double barrel. The click of the shotgun closing on two new rounds stopped the red-faced owner.

"You can stop right there," Charlie said.

"Charlie, can we just make a run for it now?" Luke said standing and brushing the glass and dirt from his shirt. His normally disheveled graying blond hair was twisted into a rat's nest and standing straight up.

"Mister, you are just in time," Charlie said, steadying the barrel on the new arrival. "We need you to open the safe and I hear you have the combination."

"You have been well informed, you asshole," the owner said, in the raspy voice of a former football coach. "Well, you are half right. I have the combination but I'll not open it for anyone with a gun. I have been robbed four times over the last nine years and I opened the safe once. They cancelled my insurance and since then I have never opened the safe and I have never given up more than $40. If I lose the money in that safe I am out of business and I'm not about to make you rich and me broke."

Charlie raised his gun and fired into the ceiling. The owner didn't react except to reach up and gently brush small chunks of plaster backwards off of his hair. A woman from the apartment above the bar looked down through the hole in her kitchen floor and started cursing Charlie.

"Another drunken asshole," she said, shaking her head. A moment later she poured a pan of hot tomato soup down the hole, hitting the bar and splashing Luke in the face.

"Damn, that's hot," Luke said wiping his face with his sleeve.

"Sorry, ma'am," Charlie said jumping aside.

"If you fire your second shot you're going to be mighty sorry," the owner said. "You'd better make it a good one because from here I can get to you before you can reload. So, you see, cowboy, it's your move."

"Don't do it, Charlie," Luke said, licking the soup off his face as water accumulated in his eyes. He came up behind Charlie and grabbed a fistful of Charlie's raincoat, pulling him toward the door. "Let's just pay for the beers and go, Charlie." He paused to look at his old friend as he had never seen him before. Finally he tilted his head toward the door and whispered, "Charlie, I'll be in the car."

"Rocky," Charlie shouted. "When you get there pop the trunk button."

"You've caught me on a benevolent day, Mr. Barman," Charlie said, after an awkward silence. "This day you will live, but I wouldn't pull that stunt with just any holdup man or you are going to be…"

Charlie couldn't remember where he was going with this outburst, so he stopped shouting and tried to look mean and determined and somewhat mentally disturbed. The owner smiled. Charlie backed toward the door, keeping his gun pointed in the direction of the end of the bar. Outside, Charlie tossed the gun in, slammed the trunk and jumped into the car.

"Okay, Rocky hit the gas! Wow, man, that was more of a rush than I had expected," Charlie said. "Did you hear them call me, Cowboy and Jesse James? Now we're making it happen instead of just being spectators. Come on, driver, show me your smooth driving moves," Charlie put on his seat belt and slapped a stunned Luke on the shoulder.

They drove with the traffic down Coliseum and turned onto West Illinois, carefully avoiding the freeways. Luke turned right on a street near Jury Park and pulled into the driveway of a small house they had rented for the month. He punched the garage door opener and drove in, shutting the door.

Charlie sat on a box and Luke lathered up Charlie's head and shaved it clean. Then Luke applied a temporary tattoo on the back of Charlie's head that read "Damned If I Will" framed in red with black and gold letters. Charlie shaved Luke's head, although Luke was well on his way to becoming bald without the assistance of a razor. They changed clothes, slipped the shotgun, their old clothing and the car license plate in a garment bag and took it out to another vehicle sitting at the curb in front of the house.

Charlie was driving with Luke lying on the floor of the back seat as the four-year-old olive Jeep pulled onto I-69 heading south.

"Hold on, Luke, we're bound for Daytona and who knows what after that."

"I wish the guy would have given us the $40," Luke said, shivering from the day's events as much as from the cold coming up through cracks in the floorboard. Charlie held the Jeep to three miles over the speed limit.

"Alright, Luke! I told you we could do it," Charlie said, letting the cool air rush over his freshly-shaved dome. "Whoa, doggies," Charlie shouted looking around at Luke, who didn't have a word to say. "The open road, here we come. Maybe we can get a job on a pit crew." Luke didn't think so but he remained quiet in the face of such enthusiasm. He had a headache and was holding his face in both hands.

Twenty minutes down I-69 Charlie saw a wall of revolving red and blue lights coming from a State Trooper roadblock a couple of miles ahead. He pulled over on the side of the road.

"What are you doing?" Luke asked.

"They're checking vehicles up ahead," Charlie said. "You've got to get out so I can get through the road block. Hurry, jump out and take the bag with you."

"Are you going to circle back to get me?" Luke asked, stepping out onto the gravel and reaching in to get the black cloth bag.

"Yes, of course, just go," Charlie said, with little intention of ever seeing his friend again. It was a flight for survival now and Charlie could feel his adrenalin pumping. This must have been what Epley had been talking about years earlier in the detention room at Perrysburg High. "Damn it, Luke, hurry or they'll get both of us."

Charlie rejoined the interstate as Luke fell and rolled down the embankment toward the woods. Charlie made it through the roadblock using one of his former company's employee badges and headed south. He lowered the window and stuck his face out in the breeze.

"How about that, Bo? How about that, Spitter?" he shouted. "Like my Jeep? Watch me, you bastards, maybe I'll drive it backwards all the way to Florida. How about that, Dale Jr.? How about that, Minnie?" Charlie blinked away the tears and felt a rush and a desperation he'd never felt before. He rolled up the window, floored the Jeep and tears came so fast he could hardly see the road driving into the dark night.

Around five in the morning he ran out of gas. Two hours before he had stopped and put his last twelve dollars in the tank. High into the mountains, he looked around at the thick Georgia pine forests on either side of the road. "Well, mister wild man, what you going to do now?" he asked out loud. First thing he did was help the Jeep down the highway grade and over a cliff. He turned and started walking down the highway even before he heard the Jeep crash far below in the valley. The night was cold in the mountains. He wondered if bobcats or cougars or coyotes ever came out of the woods to eat pedestrians where they weren't supposed to be.

A car came over the hill heading south and Charlie attempted to thumb a ride. The driver honked but sped on by. There wasn't much traffic in the middle of the night and Charlie thought he might have to walk to Daytona. He was nearly frozen and exhausted walking the mountains when a guy in an old pickup pulled over around daybreak.

"Where you goin' son?" the gray-haired driver, in a ragged John Deere hat, asked. "You ain't one of those skin heads are ya?"

"No. I'm just on my way to Daytona. Ran out of gas and money at the same time back a few miles," Charlie said.

"Bit dangerous walking these here roads, son," the driver said, sitting back in his seat with both hands on the wheel. "Animals round here are hungriest just before dawn, and besides, you can't tell what kind of people might be driving by and stop to have their way with ya. Best to not be venturin' out here of a night alone."

Charlie threw his duffel bag in the back of the truck, opened the door and stepped up to take a seat. "What made you decide to stop?" Charlie asked

"Not sure," the old man said, taking a glance over at his passenger. "Never did pick up those that ride the thumb before tonight. For one thing, I didn't think a no account snake of a man would go to all the trouble of walkin' the highway in the middle of the night. Besides, them kind is generally lazy as all get out. Son, let me ask you somethin' right off. What kind of a stupor were you in when you let some fool give you that tattoo on the back of your head? It ain't even straight."

The driver said his name was Clayton and his friends called him Clay. He wore a blue flannel shirt over his faded red tee shirt and worn jeans. Clay's little white beard bounced off his chest as he spoke. His deep-set dark eyes nearly squinted shut behind his plastic framed glasses. He talked of his life working for hire in the fields, and then for the last decade in the cotton mill near Valdosta.

"Guess I lived my life on the straight and narrow, son, you know, strict Baptist church and all. When I saw you walkin' in the dark somethin' happened in my head and I decided to do what I tell friends down at the mill to never do – pick up a hitchhiker. So, if you'd be so kind as to not rob me or shoot me and take my truck, I will get you to the Florida border and this here experiment will be a big success."

"Clay, mind if I ask how old you are?" Charlie asked, turning his head slightly to see they were moving along at 75 miles an hour.

"Seen my 82nd year come and go, son, why?"

"I was just wondering why you're still working, Clay. I mean, a man like you seems to have paid his dues. You know, time to relax a bit."

"Doctor's orders," Clay said with a sly grin, keeping his eyes on the road. "Doctor prescribed three meals a day and workin' is the only way I can afford that kind of medicine."

"You ever been arrested?" Charlie asked.

"That's a pretty private question, son," Clay said. "Once when I was young and drunk, that's about it."

"Have you ever abandoned a friend when he needed you?"

"No, can't say as I have," Clay said. "Mind telling me where you're headed with this inquiry, son?"

"Just trying to figure out where I'm going, that's all," Charlie said. "I've been in new territory for the last couple of days and it doesn't really feel like I thought it would."

"I've been driving this road part time for 10 years making deliveries and I've had some time to think," Clay said. "Far as I can determine, a person needs to figure out who they are then live that way. If you run into some extra time, figure what you are good at and find a way to share it with those who need it. Pretty simple as I see it."

"Hold on, what is this? Looks like a police barricade up ahead," Clay said, looking over at his passenger.

"Looks like it," Charlie said. "I was hoping to get to Daytona." Charlie leaned forward staring out the windshield.

"You want me to pull over to the side, son, so you can get out?" Clay asked.

"Well, what do you think Spitter? You and Bo for it? Bobby, would you and Dale Jr. be late for the race because of a little problem on the road?"

"You okay son?" Clay asked. "Do you want to get out or not?"

"No thanks, Clay," Charlie said, looking straight ahead. "You keep going and we'll give it a try. I'm just grateful for the ride."

Up on Highway 21

By Steven R. Roberts

Fujio shook himself awake at 5 am, rolled up his futon and stumbled down the dark hallway to the toilet. If he'd known what was going to happen today, Fujio wouldn't have gotten out of bed. He could feel the cold air leaking in around the window and he could see the trees bending in the wind. It was another blustery March day and the temperature inside was nearly the same as outside, minus most of the wind. Fujio took a cold bath, shaved and combed his wavy black hair. He put on clean underwear and used the one toothbrush the three guys had in the apartment. Moving back to the dark bedroom he found his uniform and shoes on the floor and got dressed. His roommates didn't have to get up for another hour. He grabbed his jacket, walked out the front door and started down Hitachi (Sunrise Street).

The late March wind rolled down the wind tunnel formed by unheated gray apartment buildings lining the street. Ironically, the winter sun would be too low in the sky to shine on Hitachi until later in the spring. Fujio pulled his jacket collar tighter and hurried to the end of the street, joining the throng of people waiting to cross at the light. Fujio was taller than the average Japanese man so he looked over the sea of black hair in front of him. He thought of it as a pulsating black wave ready to flood the intersection. When the light changed the crowd advanced directly in the path of a similar wave coming from the other side of the street. The two groups washed together in an orderly transition and they all hurried on toward their work stations.

Fujio Marubeni, a 24-year-old Osaka native, had moved with two friends, to the small industrial city of Nakagano near the western shore in the middle of Japan, seven months earlier in search of work. Fujio had been a part-time truck driver in Osaka for three years until he got in an accident and was arrested for not having a commercial license to drive. As soon as he arrived in his new city, however, he took commercial driver's training and passed the test. A week later, with certification in hand, he showed up at the right time and place and got a job driving for Okuso Petroleum. For the past six months he'd been making early morning tanker deliveries for Okuso.

Two blocks from the apartment Fujio stepped into a shop for a cup of hot tea. He sat at the window bar for a moment and held the cup in both hands. The warmth of the tea and the shop almost allowed him to stop shaking. He zipped up his jacket again, pulled up the collar and walked six more blocks to the Okuso yard.

"Good morning, Fujio," said Ichiro, a fat little man with hay-like black hair that stood on end and blew with the breeze making him look like he was leaning one way or the other even when he wasn't.

"Ichiro," Fujio said, bowing slightly. It was no secret that Ichiro had been assigned to a local route with less pay the same day that Fujio been assigned the longer route over the mountain. Ichiro had indicated on more than one occasion that he was a more experienced driver and therefore he should be assigned to the longer hauls.

Ichiro was earlier than usual this morning, undoubtedly responding to a meeting he'd had with the driver supervisor the previous day. Fujio prided himself on punctual arrival and on-time deliveries. Both were revered in the Japanese business community, however, Ichiro didn't seem to hold either in such high regard. The company also insisted that all drivers present a business-like appearance and Fujio had noticed on more than one occasion that Ichiro couldn't even keep his shirt tail in through the morning.

"Making a run over Kinpouzan this morning?" Ichiro asked, walking up to Fujio's cab from the rear. "If you've got a minute, I'd like to show you something odd about your tanker."

"What do you mean odd?" Fujio asked, looking down from the cab somewhat annoyed at what he perceived as an attempt to delay his departure. Late departure would result in a late delivery, possibly shutting down production at a large Toyota facility on the other side of the mountain. It would also get Fujio's performance reviewed. If he were removed from the Kinpouzan run, Ichiro was next in line of seniority for the route.

"It's just the right rear wheels seem out of alignment," Ichiro said. "I'm not sure but the whole axel may be loose."

"I checked the rig. It's fine, thanks," Fujio said in faked Japanese politeness. He had walked the perimeter of the rig when he arrived in accordance with company regulations. "I need to be on my way."

Fujio fired up the diesel engine sending a mushroom of black smoke high into the sky and filling the senses with a distinct petroleum fragrance. He ran through the early gears and pulled his gray 18-wheel tanker to the petroleum filling platform where he took on 14.2 kiloliters, (about 4,000 gallons). Fujio exchanged morning chatter with another driver while his tanker was being loaded. He signed for the load, pulled his rig out of the lot at 6:45 am and turned east. He was four minutes late to his scheduled departure time but he could easily make that up. This morning's run was up Highway 21, through the Kinpouzan mountain tunnel and down the other side into Toyota City. Fujio made these deliveries on Mondays, Wednesdays and Fridays, supplying Toyota's plants #2 and #5 with petroleum for filling each new vehicle with a quarter tank of gas. Depending on the weather and traffic, he would pull through the gate of the Toyota facilities at exactly 12:15 pm as specified by the customer. He'd be unloaded and on his way back to Nakagano an hour later.

He took a sip of tea and reminded himself that he needed to buy a toothbrush when he got back.

The morning fog was rolling up the side of the mountain as Fujio ran through the gears and climbed the foothills of Kinpouzan. A heavy rain started at an altitude of 1600 feet and stayed with him all the way to the tunnel, at 1900 feet. The rather light Wednesday traffic was slowed a bit by the lack of visibility but the regular drivers on Highway 21 were used to this region's morning elements.

Fujio turned up the cab heater, switched on the radio music and settled in for a four-hour run. He smiled as he thought about this coming weekend. He was going to visit his girlfriend, Yumie, back in Osaka. They'd been dating for four months before he moved. He'd been surprised and disappointed when she seemed to keep her distance after he'd been fired. But now he had a good job and he was planning to ask her to join him in Nakagano. He wouldn't expect her to move in with him right away but he was hoping they could just start over. Fujio was also looking forward to the summer months. By train, Nakagano was less than an hour from the sea and he and Yumie could spend weekends walking the beaches and drinking Sapporo, their favorite beer.

Fujio smiled when he thought of chubby Ichiro's attempt to sabotage his performance by making him late for the day's deliveries. Ichiro, like many in the world - the Americans for example - did not realize the association between fat and sloppy losers versus thin winners. Certainly, the spiky-haired one missed an important lesson of the Japanese diet along the way. He can just stuff himself to oblivion for all I care, Fujio thought, laughing to himself. He won't take this job. Without it there was no chance of his girlfriend moving to Nakagano.

The blinking yellow highway signs announced the tunnel before Fujio could see the entrance between windshield wiper strokes. He slowed to 70 kph as the tanker entered the 2.7 kilometer tunnel in the outside left lane. The tunnel was well lit and he was temporarily protected from the rain. The radio died into steady, low static.

Traffic was moving in unison when Fujio noticed the Nissan sedan in the next lane speed up. The car created a gap of about 50 meters in front of the tanker when the driver moved into Fujio's lane. Fujio saw the car spilling, or possibly leaking oil on the highway. What was this idiot doing? Now the Nissan driver was spiking the brakes. Fujio steered his rig straight and resisted braking to avoid skidding in the oil slick. He was headed straight toward the Nissan, which by now was sliding sideways across the tunnel.

Reacting involuntarily, Fujio jammed his brakes. His rig slid sideways and the tanker began to jackknife across both eastbound lanes. With 4,000 gallons of petroleum surging, the rig slid into the Nissan with a blast of sparks and metal scraping on cement. The vehicle transporter behind the tanker slammed into Fujio and the tanker started turning over on its side. One of the transporter's new vehicles broke loose from the top rack and the momentum caused it to fly up and over the belly of the tanker.

What was happening? There had been several reports of fuel trucks being hijacked in the area. Was this a botched robbery? A month before another fuel hauler's vehicle had been hijacked in a tunnel. In that instance, a car had slowed and stopped in a tunnel causing the driver to come to a stop. Hijackers pulled the driver out of the vehicle, taking over the vehicle and making off with the fuel, a theft of over $100,000 including the cost of the truck.

Fujio didn't have time to figure out what was going down in the tunnel at the top of Highway 21. Glancing quickly out the rear window of the cab, Fujio saw a flash of color as a small car flew over the midsection of his tanker. The small red Toyota came straight down into the Nissan, igniting both vehicles into a tunnel full of flames.

Yumie's smooth face appeared as a misty image on the rear window of the cab. Fujio turned and reached with one hand to touch her mouth. The window was melting and his hand adhered firmly to the glass. Fujio yelled in pain and opened his mouth to say her name but nothing came out. He tried but failed to unlatch his seat belt so he could kiss the image. Yumie's face was the last thing he saw before the cab was consumed in a ball of flames. Sliding on its side the tanker rammed the two burning vehicles into the pillars between the eastbound and westbound lanes. Sparks lit up the tunnel causing the rupturing tanker to explode in a hungry fireball, sending a blast of black smoke, flames and debris out both ends of the tunnel. The pillars cracked like thunder at the impact of the vehicles and the middle section of the tunnel started to collapse.

The morning edition of the Shimbun the next day reported there had been a tragic traffic accident in a tunnel up on Kinpouzan Mountain. A tanker driver, a car hauler driver and four other vehicle drivers had perished in the accident. An investigation into the reason for the crash was to be completed.

Just after noon the Yakuza, the Japanese mafia announced they were responsible for the accident and let it be known that the Sekiyu Transport Company, owners of the tanker, had stopped all protection money payment for their petroleum delivery routes the previous month. The police let it be known the following day that the investigation would continue since the Yakuza sometimes took credit for a disaster for their own purposes sometimes even if they were not involved.

Yumie stepped down from the train at Nakagano station the day of the memorial service for the six victims of the accident. She was met by both of Fujio's roommates and they walked to the memorial service. They were joined by the Sekiyu driver supervisor and Ichiro and the other victims' families. There were no family members attending for Fujio as his parents had stopped talking to him when he moved from Osaka.

This was a very unusual memorial service. The normal traditions of the wetting of the lips in the "Water of the Last Moment" ceremony, cremation and the picking of the bones for the urn were all waived as the collapsing mountain had buried the dead with their vehicles.

Fujio's roommates, Yumie and Ichiro had lunch after the ceremony.

"It's good to finally meet you, Ichiro" one of Fujio's roommates said as they sat down at the table. "Fujio always told us you wanted the route. I guess you will get it now."

"Well, maybe so," Ichiro said. "I guess that will have to wait until the tunnel gets fixed or the company agrees on a route around the mountain. In the meantime we'll be trying to amuse ourselves while we are out of work for a while."

"How do you amuse yourselves around here?" Yumie asked.

"Sometimes we take a train to the sea," Ichiro said. "Have you ever been to the sea?"

"Not on this side of the country."

"Would you like to give it a try?"

"I might."

Author's Note: This story is based on the chapter Highway 21 in my book, *The Share Conspiracy*, Third Printing, 2007

A Hacker Plays the Big Ones

By Steven R. Roberts

"RABBITS!" the starter said, reading from a rolled up list of tee times taken from the pocket of his baggy raincoat.

"Rabbits," he repeated, becoming more annoyed.

"Excuse me," I said, not wanting to get too close to the man for fear of getting whacked with the old putter he used as a walking stick. "Did you say Roberts?"

"That's it, lad, Rabbits," the starter said, with his weathered face and his eyes peering up through bushy gray eyebrows. "Now, I've said it three times. You're on the tee. Come along smartly now."

Bob and I picked up our clubs and walked briskly to the middle of the first tee at St. Andrews, Scotland. The first tee and the adjoining practice putting green were surrounded with would-be golfers, mostly men staring and waiting, and now they were waiting for us. The usual spitting rain had brought out the sweaters – jumpers they called them - and rain gear, as we waited for a chance to play where the legends of the game had walked since the first "Open Championship" in 1754.

The bulldog-faced starter stood close, wiping the water from his watch as I teed my ball up and took a quick practice swing. It was quite a moment, made all the more nerve-racking by my stay overnight as a guest in the Perth city jail. I wondered what else could happen when something else did. Out of the corner of my eye I noticed I had inadvertently placed my ball on a pink tee. Had that tee actually come from my pocket? This inadvertent act of disrespect would not fit with my vision of this reverent moment.

I backed away from the ball and took a white tee out of my pocket. I tried to steady my hand as I re-teed the ball and it fell off. Not wanting to look back at the impatient dark ring of observers, I re-teed and took a quick swing before it fell again. The ball took off low and sort of scooted down the left side of the fairway. It was not the shot I wanted but at least I had survived the first tee. Bob went through the process more smoothly. We grabbed our bags off the ground and trudged down the first fairway, away from the scrutiny of the lord of the tees.

And so began the story of two of the world's golf nuts who secretly harbored the universal dream that through some stroke of magic they would be able to play the historic Scottish courses responsible for creating the legends of golf lore. We hoped to play like the pros, if only for a day, or maybe a hole. The dream embraced the thin hope that our normally faulty-but-workable swings would smash drives to record distances, have our iron shots pierce through the wind to stop near the hole and, best of all, have 10-foot birdie putts disappear like chipmunks late for dinner.

Come join us if just for the smiles along the way.

The story begins in England in 1978. Bob Blackman and I had been temporarily transferred to England by our employers. He was with a drug company in Australia and I was working on a world design car for Ford Motor Company. Bob's wife, Jan, was my secretary during my tour of duty in Europe and Bob and I had met at a Ford event. Discovering our mutual interest in golf, we became friends. We vowed to get to Scotland to play the legendary courses before the end of our overseas assignments.

A year later we were on a four-day trip with tee times at the legendary championship golf courses of St. Andrews, Carnoustie, Gleneagles and Muirfield. We weren't going to be playing for a championship but we did establish a bet of five pounds each day on the medal, or total score, results. We also agreed to the bet of a new ball for the match play winner each day. The British have a quirky tradition of betting a new ball on the outcome of golf matches. Finally, birdies were worth .20 p (about a dime at the time) and a hole in one was worth a bottle of champagne. Conservative bettors, but each prize would be hard fought in our version of the Walker Cup.

We were both living in Brentwood, England, less than an hour east of London. On our first day we drove eight hours to Peebles, Scotland, just south of Edinburgh. Our hotel, the Tontine, was built in 1808, the kind of information that made me check the location of the fire escapes. Luckily, in those days they didn't construct buildings much over three or four stories high and we were on the second floor. I also noted that there was a healthy stand of bushes directly under our window.

Our tee time at Carnoustie the next morning was for 11:04 and the course was a couple of hour's drive above Edinburgh. It had been a long day and Bob went to bed early to prepare for the next day. I was a bit nervous about the next day and stayed awake for two hours listening to Bob's happy snore.

Breakfast didn't start until 8:00 am in the dining room overlooking the Tweed River. The room cost of 16 pounds, (about $35) included breakfast. The room seemed comfortable until I ran my forehead into the door jamb and realize the building was sized for the time when George III was King and Thomas Jefferson was President of a new, struggling country across the Atlantic. We got a late start but the bangers, muffin and eggs were a fitting send off for two aspiring but yet-undiscovered golfing stars.

The trip took two hours and we turned up Links Avenue for a look at our first championship challenge. At the end of the street was the quaint old golf shop (small gazebo) where we paid a modest fee of 3.75 pounds (about $8 at the time).

With the usual overcast skies and all bets in effect, the twosome of Blackman and Roberts prepare to tee off at Carnoustie. We were alone on the first tee, with the starter observing our warm up swings from his booth. A disinterested older couple and two stray dogs served as a reluctant gallery. Crack, crack and we are off.

It is possible to get lost on Scottish courses. The grasses on links grow to whatever height God allows, waving like hay in the breeze. We soon realize we couldn't even see the greens, in many cases, for our second shots, let alone hit them. We had arranged for caddies and would have been lost without them. Another feature readily noticeable at Carnoustie is the skillful and frightening use of traps. There were little annoying traps everywhere; some are small enough to hide a VW Beetle. Some traps were located in the middle of the fairways. I got in one on the first hole and had to blast out backwards. Bob decided to take a picture just as I fell flat in the sand. I threatened to expose his film if he persists with the photo thing.

After our initial excitement at being on Carnoustie, Bob and I settled down to survive. We both turned the front nine in 41, not too promising if we are going to beat Tom Watson's winning score for the British Open in 1975, but there were no broken bones or clubs so we went on. Without saying a word it was understood that all putts would be holed out. It seems the least we can do for a course that hosted five British Opens – Tommy Armour in 1931, Henry Cotton in 1937, Ben Hogan in 1953, Gary Player in 1968 and, as previously noted, Tom Watson in 1975.

I birdied number 11 and went one up. This joy lasted until 14 where Bob made a putt he had no license to make. I stumbled heading toward the gazebo clubhouse, and at the end of the first day the score was Bob 80 and Steve 81. I've lost a new ball to Bob and one in the burn on the 17th hole. I don't want to talk about it. I need a beer and a bit of a rest for tomorrow.

The next day we played 36 holes on the Gleneagles Kings and Queens courses. I'm writing this in my hotel room while Bob takes a bath. It would certainly be too bad if he drowned, but I don't want to come across as a bitter loser. It's just that he had a brilliant 74 at the difficult Kings course this morning followed by a steady 78 at the Queens this afternoon.

It's a bit hard to appreciate the beauty of this place with tears in your eyes but I must say it is spectacular. The two courses are set in the rolling Scottish hills and the clubhouse inside and out is impressive.

Toward the end of the second round, I was knackered from climbing the hills and extricating my ball and myself from the deep traps. We're both suddenly glad we didn't wait 20 more years to make this trip. The names of the holes give an extra touch to the place. Wee Bogle, Canty Lye, Devil's Creel, Waup's Nest and Blink Bonnie are indications of the dangers of the Kings course.

The turf and overall course manicure at Gleneagles was a pleasant surprise in that the conditions were similar to the finest U.S. courses. This contrasts with yesterday's seaside links course of Carnoustie with its relatively flat fairways and hard greens. On the other hand I didn't come all this way to play a U.S. course. Not to worry, because, both courses have a very different growth called "heather" throughout their roughs. If you are lucky enough to find your ball in this wiry brillo pad, we found that you needed to blast out sideways to recover. It was like trying to hit a shot out of a coil of barbed wire.

One of the other distinguishing characteristics of UK golf is the speed of play. They play a get-up-and-hit style that I found exhausting at first when we moved to England but by this time I had found it refreshing. Bob and I played Carnoustie in three hours yesterday and, excluding a one-hour break for lunch, we played 36 holes in six hours today. To add to the physical challenges of the game, these three-hour rounds are done walking, in some instances, carrying our bags. There were no golf carts on the island and caddies needed to be reserved in advance.

I already mentioned Bob's two scores for the day and purposely didn't mention mine. Bob is left handed and he has a wooden-shafted putter. If that isn't bad enough, he knocked in everything in sight for his 74 while I three-putted three times for an 80 on the Kings and 79 on the afternoon round on the Queens course. I'm now 8 shots back of Bob, who's 20 shots behind Tom Watson's winning pace. The good news is that I didn't jump off the Perth Queen's bridge as we strolled over the Tay River for dinner. What am I saying? I'm having the time of my life and tomorrow we play St. Andrews. I just need rest. I briefly considered a plan to break Bob's wooden-shafted putter over his sandy-haired head the next day.

That night we stayed in Perth. I couldn't sleep so I got up and walked across the room to Bob's bag, which was propped in the corner next to his bed. I carefully removed the wooden-shafted devil and took it out into the hall. I laid a glass from the bathroom on its side and stroked a few putts. The putter was left handed so I had to stroke the putts from the wrong side. I put the first three balls in the glass and backed up so that I was putting from the door of the room next to ours to our room door. The carpet had a slight break left to right, but I made two out of three 12-footers. This really feels good in my hands. No wonder Bob is beating me.

I backed up to another doorway and made one out of three 25-footers. Now the carpet was breaking just over a foot. Backing up again, this will be the ultimate test as to whether this thing is illegal and I should confiscate it. I'm stroking the first 50-footer when an older lady in her white nightgown comes out of one of the rooms along the putting path. I've got my head down, concentrating on making a smooth stroke; I got a chill up my neck realizing the ball was on pace and line perfectly toward the hole. I looked up to see the lady rubbing her eyes as she stepped on the ball and sprawled out across the hallway. Her nightgown billowed like a small parachute as she screamed and fell to the slightly-slanted hallway carpeting.

"Oh, ma'am, I'm so sorry," I said, hurrying to her side.

"I heard a scream and opened my door to find this man standing over this poor woman," the man from the other side of the hall said to the constable. "He was standing there with a red face in his whitey tidy undershorts and a club in his hand. My friend next door and I blocked his attempts to get to his room until you got here, Constable."

Bob had heard the commotion in the hall and he'd brought my trousers out to me but it was too late.

So, that's how the day I had looked forward to for so long got started. The day I was scheduled to play St. Andrews began with breakfast in the Perth city jail.

"How you doing?" Bob asked, coming to the visitor's room about 8:30 that morning.

"Oh, God, Bob, it's lucky we got a later tee time," I said. "Can you get me out in time?"

"I'll see. I suppose you have some explanation as to what you were doing walking the halls in your skivvies with my putter at 3:20 in the morning?" Bob asked.

"Never mind that right now," I said. "We can talk about it on the long drive home in a couple of days."

"Well, I don't know what happened with that woman or my putter, but I've called St. Andrews and changed our hotel reservation for tonight to separate rooms."

"You didn't."

"Yes. Besides, you snore."

"Whatever. Just get me out of here in time to hit a few practice balls and I'll be okay."

"I'm meeting with the constable in 10 minutes," Bob said. "Let's hope I can convince him you were doing something rational out there in that hallway. Do you have any words to help me make him understand?"

"No. Just get me out of here."

Two hours later, Bob was driving as we turned off the main street in St. Andrews onto narrow Links Avenue. I put on my golf shoes as Bob drove past the Old Niblick Restaurant and pulled into the small parking lot 12 minutes before our tee time of 1:33 pm.

Bob and I hadn't had much to say to each other on the trip down from Perth, but the normal golf babble broke out as we saw the Royal and Ancient Clubhouse and sensed the moment was near.

"What if we take a divot?" I asked.

"You replace it. What else?" Bob said.

"I was just imagining a juicy chunk of this place framed, under glass, hermetically sealed and hanging in my den back home," I said.

"I think you may be having a histrionic, historic fit," Bob said.

He was right. I needed to pull myself together and get mentally tough for the match of the day. There was a lot of ground to make up on Bob and the wooden-shafted devil.

I leaned over the first tee rail and held out the money to pay for the greens fees.

"Step baack, lod," the cashier man said. "I'll tull ya when ya kin pie." The cashier and the starter were definitely in control of when and if those of us standing in the misty rain could play.

George III could have used these guys. The King outlawed the game twice during his reign. Even in those days politicians would stoop to any level for the ladies' approval.

After the setback involving a pink tee, and after I hit my second shot into the Swilcan Burn that runs in front of the first green, we were on our way. I took a double-bogie six on number one and thought I understood better why they call the stream a burn.

The course was essentially a narrow strip of land along the sea, with the front nine going out and the second nine coming back. Some of the greens were so big they were used for a hole going out on one half of the green and a pin on the other side of the green for the hole coming back. Some fairways were also shared and, in fact, two of the fairways crossed each other.

My round for the day seemed almost of secondary importance as I drank in the history and stark beauty of the course jammed against the rugged sea. I managed to concentrate long enough to birdie 14 and 15; Bob birdied 3 and 12. In the end I had some disasters and finished with an 81 while the devil and his friend had a steady 78. It just goes to show, you must be very careful in choosing your traveling friends. Next time I'm going to find somebody 75 years old with a bad back and enough social grace to give me a few three-footers.

In no time at all, it hit me that the long-awaited round was going to be over too soon. The mist had stopped by the time we looked down the fairway from the 17th tee. The tee shot on the notoriously difficult hole must start down the left side of the fairway and fade or go over the edge of the hotel positioned helplessly at the corner of the dogleg. We navigated the corner successfully but noticed many pock marks in the side of the building from less fortunate.

Bob and I walked up on the 18th tee just 2 hours and 45 minutes after teeing off. Off to our left, we could see the first tee was still crowded with players anxious to chase their dreams. I walked tall, visualizing the Championship crowds with thousands of spectators standing along Golf Avenue to the right and the grandstands behind the square green holding 8,000 fans on tournament Sunday. This was the final hole and I had a chance to win the British Open by besting Palmer and Nicklaus by a stroke. I needed only a par on the final hole. I visualized a par because there was no way I could birdie the hole in front of thousands of people and all of the press and TV crews jammed against the ropes. Actually, Doug Sanders walked up to his drive the final day in 1972 needing only a par to win. I looked for Sanders' divot but it had healed over.

Bob and I were both over the road that bisects the hole and Bob was away. Let me clarify. I out-drove good old Bob. He hit a pitch and run shot that reached the front edge of the green.

For me, it was enough of a test just to pull the club back for the second shot. I selected a wedge and went down through the green sod, soaked by rain the night before while I had been incarcerated. My shot took off high but was pulled to the left, just catching the edge of the large green. The crowd went nuts, or so it seemed. As I walked forward to pick up the turf and return it to its honored place, I took one last look back at St. Andrews.

"I'll be back someday, old man by the sea," I said out loud. "You will know me. Next time I'll have a left-handed, wooden-shafted putter and you won't have a chance."

Bob struck his 110-foot putt well with that stupid-looking putter. The ball hit the hole and stopped two inches away. The two people clapping as they walked along the railing behind the green represented the 20,000 there each time this course hosts the Open Championship.

If I could somehow sneak in my 32-footer, I could pull within five shots of the young, albeit cheating, left-handed Australian. My putt was pure and in all the way but somehow hit the lip and spun out. The couple along the rail let out an "ohuuu" in unison. Is there no justice? As I lined up the curling two-footer return putt, I remembered that Doug Sanders had this same putt to best Jack Nicklaus and win the championship in 1972. The official silver smith was already carving his first name in the trophy when the unbelievable happened. Sanders missed the short putt. He would go on to lose the playoff with Nicklaus the next day.

Out of respect for the history of the game, I too missed the very same two-footer. I could have made it if I had wanted to. Honest, I could have.

The final day of competition was at Muirfield Golf Club near Scotland's southern border. It's officially known as the "Company of Honorable Gentlemen from Edinburg" and it was the only private club we attempted to play. We arrived to find only one car in the parking lot.

"Could you direct us to the Pro Shop?" I asked the club secretary.

"Muirfield da noot hoov a pru ship," (or a pro for that matter), he said. "Ya kin buy bells un tees if ya moost." There you have the Scottish disdain for things commercial. There were no souvenir shirts, hats, gloves or bag tags for sale at Muirfield. One imagines any money prize awarded at the Open Championship to be held in 1980 will be slipped under the winner's door in a plain white envelope.

Standing in front of the clubhouse you can see across the rugged links course to the sea. Some 40 miles north across the Firth of Forth lies yesterday's winner, St. Andrews, and another 40 miles north across the Tay River is the rugged Carnoustie.

Here's just a word about the course. Bob and I decided it would be tough on a calm day but the gales blow steadily all day off the sea without relief. Muirfield members say if there was a day without wind they wouldn't know what to lean against.

The rough is knee high everywhere you look except for the thin strips of the fairways. Some players think there may be whole families living in the tall grass. Nicklaus used his driver only four times per round in winning in 1966. But as tough as the course was tee to green, the greens were tougher. On the third hole my caddie, another of the weathered veteran survivors of the sea breezes, spent some time telling me exactly how my uphill 30-footer broke. I steadied myself over the ball and took a stroke which traveled to the crest of the break and stopped. As I took a step forward, the ball turned, slowly rolling back down the hill coming to rest at my feet. My caddie turned to look out at the sea. He didn't bother to read my putts again for the rest of the round.

It was a tough battle that day and Bob kept up the pressure giving me little chance of catching him in our match. By the time we got to the 17th hole, a 530-yard par 5, I was looking for an appropriate climactic stage for the finishing moments of the competition. This hole would most likely play a defining moment in the championship which was scheduled for the 1980 Open.

Bob's caddie advised that in some wind conditions the par five is reachable in two. On my second shot, I swung a three wood with both feet off the ground and was able to reach the front of the green. Bob got lucky and put his second shot 60 feet from the pin. He two-putted for a birdie. I won't bore you with the details, but I managed to sink a two-footer for my six.

Finishing off the round with pars, we took some comfort in the fact that Gary Player took a double bogie six on the final hole to win the Open Championship in 1958.

We packed up our wet gear and said goodbye to four days of soaking in the adventure of the best the game had to offer. On the drive home that afternoon and evening, Bob and I played the "if only" game, a favorite of all golfers. This technique allowed us to imagine away five or six shots a round. Looking back over the four rounds, each course had the devil buried inside its character. Carnoustie was a weathered Scottish seaman's face; Gleneagles was a soft, classy lassie with curves in the right places; St. Andrews was the ceremonial lord of the manor with understated British strength and style; and Muirfield was a wicked woman with her fringed skirt flapping in the breeze – aggravating because you suspect she might be easy for some but not for you.

We also distributed the prizes on the drive home. Bob beat me two rounds and we tied for two, so he won ten pounds and six golf balls. He had six birdies during the week compared to my four, so Bandit Bob won another 40 pence. Luckily, he didn't have any eagles or holes in one.

I was driving when we passed the Nottingham Forest exit about halfway home. I slowed down to let a sheriff's car pass me in hot pursuit. I supposed he was looking for Robin Hood. The sheriff would be well advised, I thought, to check out the sandy-haired hood sitting in the dark, chuckling quietly in the passenger seat of my car.

I was also smiling. If Bob doesn't play again for a week he is going to have a real surprise. Before we loaded up at Muirfield, I found a city of termites under the woodwork in the hotel. I'd spent half the night collecting the squiggly little termite biters and I was able to poke the putter shaft through the bag and slide it down the shaft, finally securing the bag to the shaft midway with tape. In a week Bob will find only a club head, grip and a pile of sawdust after the little beasties have a go at that tasty shaft.

But alas, Bob and I have had a week of living out a dream. We have walked the same fairways and greens that have been walked for centuries of golfers, from the founding fathers of the game to the stars of recent years. No other sport provides its fans such an opportunity to so closely assimilate the physical challenges of its major championships. The average amateur baseball player is not permitted to walk to the pitcher's mound in Yankee Stadium and pitch three innings, and the weekend football nut cannot play running back at Heinz Field stadium facing the Pittsburgh Steelers. But we stood on the same spot on the 17th fairway at St. Andrews and faced the same wind off the Firth of Forth that has humbled the greats of the game for centuries. All the more is the hacker's thrill if he somehow carries his ball over the trap and keeps it from bouncing over the green onto the road.

So, that's my story from a week in the middle of October, 1979. Having read this only slightly-exaggerated report on our trip, you are exempt from listening to my telling of the story in the event we run into each other at a cocktail party somewhere down the road. But if after a few drinks the conversation turns to lifelong dreams, my answer will be clear. There are many more courses out there to be concurred. But, do me a favor. Bob is still raw over the mysterious pulverizing of his wooden shaft. If he's around, just don't say anything about another trip.

Author's note: This story was originally written two months after the trip. I sent a copy to my former teammate at college and attached is a reproduction of his response. He finished second to Tom Watson at Muirfield in 1980. I should have been on the bag and helped him read those tricky greens.

Jack Nicklaus

June 16, 1980

Mr. Steven R. Roberts
35 Priests Lane
Brentwood,
Essex,
England

Dear Steve,

Please accept my apologies for not answering your letter sooner, but as you know, I have been traveling a bit lately.

I wanted to thank you for the copy of your story about your visit to Carnoustie, Gleneagles, St Andrews and Muirfield. I certainly enjoyed reading it ...made me more anxious than ever to be back at Muirfield in July.

Thanks again, Steve, for the nice gesture.

Best Regards

-signed-

Jack Nicklaus

1208 U.S. Hwy #1 North Palm Beach, Florida,33408

Final Moments

The quotes from Poe and Hawthorne in the front of the book gave guidance on the form, length, power and purpose of the short story. The intent of the stories included here has been to bring the form to life for entertainment, information and inspiration. I hope you found one or more stories that help you forget about the world and its problems for an hour or so. For variety, I also added a few poems and short farcical pieces to lighten the serious Moments.

Undoubtedly you were able to tell the difference between the real and whimsical stories. In case you missed it, however, Jonah Whittaker really didn't find the secret potion to allow him to join the NBA. If you see North Korea's president, Kim Jong il, you may want to let him know. Further, Fujio was not killed in the explosion that happened up on Highway 21. The termites, however, are still struggling to digest Bob's stupid putter shaft.

Thanks again to the guest storytellers who contributed variety of style and perspective. Please check out their web sites for more information on their books and other writings.

I'm currently working on a second in the series of Moments anthologies. If you have an incident that turned the course of your life or the life of someone you know, contact me for consideration at srandjfroberts@aol.com. No promises, but your story could end up in a future edition of Moments. Check out my web site www.steverroberts.com for updates on Moments Book II.

Books By Steven R. Roberts

Rhythm and Rhyme Lifetime
A Poet and Songwriter's Inspiration

Twenty-Nine Months
A Twenty-Year Fight with Cancer and Its Consequences

The Share Conspiracy
Motown Vigilantes Fight Back Against
Japanese Auto Invasion

Brothers Popovic
Escape From Croatia
Based On a True Story

A Freak's Journey
The Life and Times of a Six Year Old Circus Runaway
Based On a True Story

The Moment It All Changed
Short Stories of Adventure, Inspiration, Epiphany
Humor and Surprise

Also see web site, www.steverroberts.com for information on Steve's other writings including contributions to anthologies, *Bedpan Banter, The MacGuffin* and *Thank God I.*

About The Author

Steven R. Roberts

Moment is Steve's sixth book, a combination of fictional and true short stories. The stories contained in this anthology have been selected for their vibrant characters, fit with the theme model and for their potential entertainment value. The intent was to include stories by Steve and his guest writers for a wide variety of tastes.

Steve is a veteran of the automotive industry in Detroit and Europe and is currently a consultant to small businesses. He is also Chairman of the Board and CEO of the Dearborn Library Foundation. Steve conducts writing workshops and runs writers' clubs in Michigan and Florida.

The author and his wife, Jane, live in Dearborn, Michigan, and have four married children as well as 11 grandchildren. More information can be obtained on Steve's writings at his web site: www.steverroberts.com.